The Indie Yuletide Tales
A Festive Collective

A diverse collection of stories showcasing some of the best indie authors on the market. Filled with heart-warming romance, mysterious humor, sinister, supernatural thrills and tearful sorrow, this anthology has something for everyone. So snuggle up with a warm glass of mulled wine and join us for the festivities, while we lift your spirit, tickle your fancy and rattle your bones.

ISBN-13:978-1493747917
ISBN-10:1493747916

Copyright Retained By Authors
Cover Art by Book Birdy Designs

The Indie Collaboration grew out of a group of like minded independent authors. Together, we decided to show the world how great works of fiction can be created without the involvement of any large publishing companies; creating a direct channel between ourselves and our readers is of the utmost importance to us. Each author has freely donated their time and work and are committed to the Indie Collaboration's cause of:
*Offering the best of indie authors
in bite size pieces for free.*
We hope you enjoy our books.

Contents

- Page 4. Christmas Spirit by Sonya C. Dodd
- Page 15. The Best Gift Ever by Shemeka Mitchell
- Page 29. He Sees You When You're Sleeping by D.C Rogers
- Page 40. Peter's Wish by William O'Brien
- Page 41. The Spirits of Christmas by Peter John
- Page 54. Christmas Hope by Jim Murdoch
- Page 66. The Case of The Shiny Red Gift Box by Chris Raven
- Page 74. Glimpse by William O'Brien
- Page 75. The Perfect Gift by Carolyn Bennett
- Page 87. On Christmas Day by Alan Hardy
- Page 102. A Sacred Star by Sheryl Seal
- Page 112. True Heart by William O'Brien
- Page 113. The Christmas Heart by Kristina Blasen
- Page 121. This Christmas by The Greatest Poet Alive
- Page 129. Secret Santa By Madhu Kalyan Mattaparthi
- Page 135. Time To Go by William O'Brien
- Page 136. About The Authors
- Page 163. Also By The Indie Collaboration

Christmas Spirit
By
Sonya C. Dodd

"I don't see the point in us having a tree if we've nothing to put under it," Jack sighed. It was the same every year and it didn't get any easier saying no to Janice and their son, Tom.

Everything had been wonderful when he'd been in work. They could have had a Christmas tree in every bloody room then, if they'd wanted it. But then the crash had happened and slowly Jack had watched his world crumble around him.

He was thankful for his small family and it had been great, the way they hadn't blamed him for anything but just accepted the change in their lifestyle.

Then, when the house was sold because they could no longer afford the crippling mortgage payments, neither of them had uttered a word against him when they'd moved out of town to live in the back of beyond where they could at least afford the meagre rent on their single-storey home.

Jack used the term 'home' loosely and was fully aware that it was the people inside who made a house a home; but this ramshackle dump, where the wind tore through the gaps between the window frames and brickwork, was not what he had envisaged for them.

Work was still elusive and he made money where he could, doing odd jobs for anyone who took pity on him. Swallowing his pride had come along with the house move and Jack knew he couldn't afford to be proud if he was going to continue putting food on their table.

Now with Christmas approaching quickly, the shame and disappointment of not being able to give his family the kind of festive season they deserved was playing constantly on Jack's mind.

He could see the disappointment in Tom's face whenever an advertisement came on the television for the latest toy or gadget. The screen seemed to be permanently ablaze with colourful scenes and a chorus of carols or festive songs.

Aged eleven, Tom was acutely aware of what was going on around him and Jack could only admire his son's dignified silence as he stopped himself from whining constantly as many others would have.

Losing sleep and patience, Jack knew his anxiety was all down to Christmas and he wished they could just sleep through the approaching holiday until it was all over and dull normality was resumed.

Jack looked at Janice's hopeful face. He was sure she was aging before his eyes and knew it was down to the life he was responsible for presenting them with. He didn't understand why she stuck it out with him. She was a beautiful woman and she would be quite within her rights to leave him, taking Tom with her to go and find a man who deserved them.

"I wish we could, honey, but it'll only make it harder for Tom on Christmas Day if we have a tree sitting in here." Jack looked around the tiny sitting room/kitchen. Despite Janice's efforts to decorate the place when they had moved in, there was already evidence of damp on the walls and nothing prevented the curtains from swaying with the breeze coming in from the chilly December evening outside.

"We don't mind about the presents," Janice began quietly. "We've told you that. I just think it would cheer the place up a bit and make us a little more like everyone else."

Jack snorted. "Like everyone else?" He looked at her incredulously. "Look around you, love, 'cos this is what you've got to get used to. We are not like everyone else so a bloody tree in a pot isn't gonna make us otherwise."

Janice made a grab at her handbag, which was lying on the table, and pulled it resolutely over her shoulder. "Your self-pity is the worst thing, Jack. I think Tom and I have done a brilliant job of supporting you and all I'm asking for is a small token to help us celebrate along with everyone else. I don't expect something like they have in Trafalgar Square and we're not asking you for presents. Just get over yourself Jack and open your eyes to the world around you, before it disappears."

For a moment Janice stood watching him, breathless; then she turned on her heel and Jack watched helplessly as she marched out of the house, slamming the door behind her.

He was stunned. Janice was always so calm and easy-going. Jack couldn't recall when he had ever heard her raise her voice to him or Tom. Staring at the closed door, Jack struggled to take in his wife's words.

Was that how she really saw him? Tom too? She'd made it sound as though they were both getting fed up with him. Would they really go? He shook his head slowly and let it drop onto his open hands.

He'd never been a bad person but Jack could only see their current state as something he'd brought upon them all. He was shocked to think Janice saw him as self-pitying. Okay, he knew his manliness had taken a pretty hefty knock with the length of time he'd been out of work now, and with the way they had been forced to live in this hell-hole; but Jack was aghast that his family might think of him as pitiful or worthless.

Slowly, Jack stood up and slipped his arms into the sleeves of his jacket. If he knew Janice, she'd be on her way to her mother's now. Jack could picture the smug way his mother-in-law would greet her daughter in an 'I told you so' fashion, before pouring her a large glass of wine.

Janice had always been close to her mother, since her father had died when she was still a child, but there had never been any attempt by Janice's mother to conceal her impression that Jack wasn't good enough for her daughter. And now he'd finally managed to prove she had been right all along.

However, Jack wasn't going to let Janice and his son just walk out of his life without a fight. He might not be able to give them much, but if it was a tree Janice wanted, then it would be a tree she would get.

Pulling his beanie down over his ears and slipping his hands into his sheepskin gloves, Jack pulled the door shut and braced himself to face the cold night air.

The wind was biting and his cheeks were burning at once. Cursing under his breath, Jack stepped outside and pulled the door quickly closed behind him.

Hesitating, he looked around, listening to the silence and trying to formulate some plan of action which might get him back inside the relatively warm house as soon as possible.

Their house bordered a small plantation with a mixture of deciduous and coniferous trees and Jack was sure the landowner wouldn't miss just one small tree. He took his pickaxe from the shed and, with it slung over his shoulder, Jack climbed over the low wire fence, to go in search of something he could slay with his small axe.

Never having liked the idea of a real Christmas tree, Jack hated the sound of his axe striking the trunk of the feeble-looking pine tree. Of course, there was no way he could afford to buy an artificial one but he couldn't rid himself of the feeling he was murdering this helpless specimen.

With the tree lying murdered on the ground by his feet,

Jack picked up the severed end and dragged it behind him, back to the house.

In the dim light of the yard he looked down at the tree and realised he'd need something to stand it in if he was going to have it ready for when Janice got home. Returning the axe to the shed, Jack rummaged around in the dark until he discovered an old, plastic bucket.

Just as he was closing the shed door, Jack thought he heard a sneeze. He looked around him: Did foxes sneeze? He wondered.

With the bucket and tree in hand, Jack dismissed the sound and went inside. It was then he realised he needed some soil in the bucket to support the tree. He leant the tree in the corner of the room and took the bucket back outside.

This was going to be fun, he thought, tapping a spade against the solid, frozen ground. Just as he struck the ground again, this time with a little more force, Jack heard a sneeze again.

He looked round and called out: "Hello?"

There was no sound, not even a scurrying of small animal feet. All Jack could hear was the wind rustling in the trees and the distant buzz of traffic, heading in and out of the city.

As he raised his spade in the air, this time Jack heard the distinct noise of a human cough. The spade landed with a clatter.

"Who's there?" Jack called, trying to sound braver than he felt.

Once more there was no response. Fed up with the build-up of events on an evening where he had assumed he'd be in front of the television with his wife, whilst their son was on a sleepover at a friend's house, Jack marched into the kitchen and grabbed the torch from underneath the kitchen sink.

Outside again, he shone the flashlight around the empty yard. As he was about to turn the light off and return inside, Jack thought he ought to check the other side of the shed, just to put his mind at rest.

With the beam of light on the muddy ground, it was the dirty, battered black shoes, he saw first. Following the line of the body with his torch, Jack noted the sorry state of the black trousers covering the skinny legs. The rest of the body was hidden by the shed and Jack realised he was holding his breath as he slowly turned to view the figure.

The man was sitting on the hard, cold ground. He wore a black jacket, which had seen better days and his head was slumped forward. Glad he knew the man was alive from the sounds he'd made earlier, Jack hesitated.

His head was slumped forward and his face covered by the grey, shoulder length hair. Surprised he hadn't already died of frost bite, Jack wondered how long the guy had been here, unnoticed.

"You okay?" Jack asked.

There was no reply but ever so slowly, the man raised his head until Jack was looking into the blackest pair of eyes he had ever seen. The pale skin and grey hair were quite a contrast to the black and were the only parts of the man which would have been visible if it hadn't been for Jack's torch.

Time seemed to stand still as they gazed at each other. Jack assumed he must be some vagrant, looking for a sheltered spot for the night. He realised he felt sorry for the guy. It was close to Christmas, freezing cold and this person looked too old and thin to be out in this bitter weather. Jack might have felt down and out himself, but he knew he was rich compared to this character.

"It's gonna be a cold one," Jack said, looking up at the starry sky as he spoke. "You'll catch your death out here."

The stranger's eyes seemed to sparkle at the sound of Jack's voice and a small smile crept onto his dry, narrow lips.

"Can I at least make you a hot drink?" Jack suggested. "It's not much, but there's a bit of stew left over from dinner too. We were going to have it tomorrow but you're welcome to it." He knew he was stuttering and talking too much, but Jack felt an overwhelming desire to help this man who looked even more unfortunate than he was.

As the man glanced around him, as if to find some way of getting himself up, Jack stepped forward and reached round his body to help him to his feet. Despite the large jacket, Jack could feel how thin the man was and how ill-prepared for the wintry night his clothes were.

Leading the way into the house, Jack indicated a chair for the man to sit in and set about making a mug of tea and warming the stew on the stove.

There was no conversation but Jack could sense the man watching him. It was strange how he felt nervous in his own home, under the scrutiny of this feeble visitor.

Then, with the steaming vessels on the table, it was Jack's turn to watch as the man silently, but hurriedly, devoured both the food and tea. Jack smiled to see the pleasure such a small token could bring to another person.

"You take the chair by the fire now," Jack told him as the spoon clattered into the empty bowl. "You look as though you could do with warming up."

"Thank you," the stranger replied as he shuffled from one chair to another.

Surprised by the softness of his voice, Jack tidied the remnants of the meal away, not wishing to bombard his visitor with too many questions at once.

When he was done, Jack took a chair opposite the man and they eyed each other in silence.

After a while, despite the easy air, Jack felt he should say something. "Do you come from around here?"

"Here, there, everywhere," the man replied lightly.

"A bit of a traveller?"

"You could say that." Although his lips moved and there was light in his eyes, you would have thought he was a statue the way his body remained motionless and his face still, Jack noticed.

"I'm sure you could find better shelter in the city," Jack said. "It can't be right for a person to have to live rough when the temperature is this cold."

"I don't mind the cold," the stranger replied. "Don't feel it after a while."

Jack shifted in his seat. The guy seemed harmless but there was something odd about him which Jack couldn't put his finger on. Anyone else would have been chatting or huddled in front of the fire, which provided the only warmth in the room; but this guy was like a mannequin, happy to accept Jack's hospitality yet giving nothing of himself away.

He didn't feel threatened in any way by the stranger but Jack felt as if he was under scrutiny.

"Look, I've got to do something with this tree," Jack said, nodding at the forgotten Christmas tree in the corner; "but you're welcome to remain by the fire if you'd like."

The stranger smiled and closed his eyes.

Laughing quietly to himself, Jack got up and went outside to fetch the bucket. It took him quite a while to get enough soil into the pail before he returned into the house. By the time he did, he was sweating from the effort and he saw his guest was sleeping peacefully in the chair.

Even as Jack moved around the room, putting the tree in its resting place and organising the chairs around their new centre-piece, the man seemed oblivious to his presence.

Jack glanced at his watch. It was nearly eleven. It looked like Janice must be staying at her mother's for the night, he realised. Feeling weary himself, Jack stretched and yawned. He chewed his lip as he surveyed his guest. There seemed no harm in letting him remain where he was. He looked incapable of murdering him in his sleep, so Jack left a lamp on in the corner of the room and took himself off to bed.

The following morning, when Jack woke up, the first thing he did was to stretch his arm out across the bed. Discovering he was alone, he sighed and opened his eyes, looking at the empty space where Janice should have been. Please don't let her leave me at Christmas, he thought to himself miserably.

Just then he heard the sound of car brakes, followed swiftly by a closing door. Janice! Jack realised, her mum must have paid for a taxi.

Suddenly recalling his evening visitor, Jack leapt out of bed. He had no idea how his wife would react to seeing a random waif and stray sitting in their front room, but he was positive it wouldn't be a great reception, even if the guy was still there.

He pulled on a pair of boxer shorts, grabbed his dressing gown and was just entering the sitting room as Janice appeared through the front door.

Their eyes met immediately but each remained silent as they took in their surroundings. At once Jack realised his guest was gone and quietly sighed in relief. But there was much more to be concerned about at that moment than what had happened to the man he'd given food and shelter to.

Whilst his thoughts were racing, Janice launched herself

into his arms, knocking him backwards into the door in her enthusiasm. "I knew you wouldn't let us down. I'm sorry I was such a bitch yesterday but how on earth did you manage all this on your own?"

Jack stood helplessly with his mouth open, unable to formulate any kind of explanation. Of course he was relieved Janice had come home and to be back in her good books, but he had no idea how to explain the transformation to their sitting room.

The tree he had brought in was decorated and seemed to have been given a new burst of life with the fairy lights and star on top. Underneath the tree was an array of presents taking up so much space, they were spilling into the room.

Christmas decorations hung from the ceiling and walls making their home look like Santa's grotto.

Janice let go of him and went into the kitchen, pulling the fridge door open. The shelves were stacked with festive goodies, surrounding an enormous turkey. Unable to believe what they were seeing, Jack watched as Janice went from one cupboard to the next, opening doors and then pausing to take in the full shelves.

When the last cupboard stood open, Janice turned to face her husband. "How did you afford this, Jack? Please tell me we're not in debt for all this, just to keep me happy."

He could understand her concerns, Jack was mystified himself but he shook his head quickly. "I wish I could take the credit for this but I have no idea where it all came from. I got the tree, but this wasn't here when I went to bed last night," he assured her.

Janice gave a small, worried laugh. "Then how Jack? How did it get here?"

He walked towards her, still marvelling at the scene surrounding them. Resting his hands on her hips, Jack looked at her: "There was this old guy; he was sitting by our shed. I felt sorry for him and invited him in."

"He was a tramp?" Janice interrupted him.

"Looked like it. It was freezing out there, so I brought him in and gave him something to eat and drink and left him sleeping by the fire when I went to bed. That was it until I woke up this morning and you turned up."

"Do you think he had something to do with this?" she asked slowly.

"I don't see how. He was old and scrawny, hardly capable of doing all this on his own," Jack remarked.

"Maybe he could perform magic," Janice said, smiling.

"What? Like Father Christmas?"

THE END
2013 Sonya C. Dodd

The Best Gift Ever
By
Shemeka Mitchell

Tahara sat in the dark trying to come up with some sort of plan. Instead, her mind was blank. All she felt like doing was crying. No matter how hard she tried, things always managed to fall apart around her feet. How could she teach her children to be successful adults when she could hardly keep food on the table and the utilities on? As she continued sitting there wondering how she was going to come up with the money to pay the bill, she heard a car pull up.

She opened the door without looking out the window. She smelled his cologne as soon as he entered the house.

"Hello Tahara, how are you?"

"Hi Mike, I'm great. How are you?" She attempted to put on a happy face for his benefit. She didn't want him to worry about his son staying with a weak and wimpy woman. She had to show him that she was responsible.

She knew that Mike saw the sadness in her eyes. She did a nice job of trying to cover it up, but he'd known her too long for it to go unnoticed by him.

***

"Why don't you tell me what is really going on?" he said as he dropped down on the couch. The living room was dark. He figured that her daughter was in the bed and the boys were in the room probably playing video games.

Mike had been on his way to club with his friends. With him being a single father, he did not have a lot of time for hanging out with his friends. They were always trying to get him to hook up with different women and he wasn't really into all of that. He was ready to settle down and have a family, a complete family. As of yet, however, he was still single. And it was thanks to his son's mother who felt like being a mom was cramping her style. So, she left him and their son to move to New York and live the city life. His priorities had changed drastically and his friends couldn't seem to understand that. His main focus was taking care of his boy. That is how he met Tahara, through their boys. They had been best friends for a while and had been in the same class since the third grade. They were like brothers. In fact, when people saw them out in public, they automatically assumed that they were. Mike and Tahara had managed to form a budding friendship because of the time that they spent together. Little did Tahara know, Mike's feelings for her were past that of just a friendship. He wanted so much more, but he didn't quite know how to approach her. He knew that she was damaged, but he was willing to take a chance and show her how good they could be together. He adored spending time with her. They always had a great time on their outings with the kids. Lately he had begun to imagine building a life with her. When they went out they made a stunning couple. She may not have realized it, but he did. He saw the looks people gave them, the smiles at seeing them together. They fit. She was around 5'4 to his 6 feet. Her skin was the color of milk chocolate and he so desperately wanted to taste her. Her body was voluptuous and thick in all of the right places. Her curves were dangerous and he wanted to explore each and every one of them. He just didn't know how to tell her without scaring her off.

"Everything is good. I told you that. I'm just thinking about Christmas and how we are going to celebrate it." Which wasn't a complete lie, she was thinking or better yet, praying that the utility company wouldn't turn her lights off at Christmas time.

"Are you sure? You know you can talk to me about anything, right?" He wanted her to open up to him and let him in. He knew that she was stressed majority of the time. With hardly any help from her children's father, she was handling it all on her own. He admired the strength and dedication she had for her family.

"I'm sure. Would you like something to drink?" She had to change the subject before everything spilled out and he knew it. Mike was a single parent also, but the difference was that he had a career. He made a decent enough living to provide for his family. Tahara did not feel like being judged by him, nor anyone else for that matter. He would never do that to her, but he knew that was how she felt because she'd told him that on plenty of occasions.

While she was in the kitchen getting the drinks, he noticed a notebook lying open on the end table. His curiosity got the best of him as he glanced at the paper. It looked like it was a budget sheet or something. He moved closer so that he could get a better look. He guessed this was what was wrong with her. He looked at the figures and knew without a doubt that this right here was the problem. She was up to her head with bills and wouldn't have any money for gifts. He couldn't understand why she wouldn't come to him if things were this bad. He wouldn't mind helping her out. She was precious to him, a true friend. Plus, his son spent plenty of hours here. More than he actually spent at home, if Mike was honest about it.

Tahara walked back into the living room and handed him the drink.

"I thought you were on your way out?" she asked as she sat down beside him.

"I was but the closer I got to the place, the more I

wanted to be anywhere else besides there."

"And what made you choose to come here?"

"I really didn't feel like being alone and my son is already here. It seemed like a good idea at the time. I was thinking that we could watch a few movies, listen to some music. You know, just enjoy one another's company for a little while." He watched her reaction to his words, hoping to gather some sort of inkling about how she felt towards him.

"I'm glad you came back. I really didn't need to be alone myself," she admitted to him.

"So tell me, why are you still single?"

"I haven't found that one yet." She said as she turned her body to face him.

"Are you one of those picky females with the long list of requirements?" He already knew for a fact that she was not that way.

"Whatever Mike, you know better. I cannot believe that it is almost Christmas," she exclaimed as she sat back on the sofa. Her body was stiff and he knew that she was mentally exhausted.

"Have you done your shopping yet?" he asked even though he knew that she didn't have the money for it.

"No, not yet." Her voice was low, almost a whisper.

"What are you waiting on? You know everything is going to be gone soon."

"I'll get to it eventually," she said and changed the subject, "What do you want to watch, a chick flick, horror, comedy, holiday movie, what?" she asked him as she browsed through the DVDs?

"I'm cool with whatever you pick. I know you love those scary movies." Mike said.

"Sure do. Okay, let's watch Insidious." She said as she

picked out the movie from the pile.
***

Her earlier despair had slowly tapered away thanks to Mike. He was a godsend. His presence always lifted her spirits in a major way. She could not imagine why he was still single. He was a handsome man. He had hazel eyes and lashes that women would kill for. His skin was smooth and the color of honey. He was always playing ball with the boys or doing some sort of physical activity and his body was the result of it. It was rock hard in all of the right places. He had deep dimples in both cheeks that she loved playing with. He always laughed when she stuck her finger in his dimples when they showed up. She was sure he could get any woman he wanted. When they were out together, she always saw women looking his way. Once when they were at a pizza joint, a lady cornered her in the restroom and asked if they were a couple. When she told the woman they were just friends, the woman wrote her name and number on a napkin and begged her to give it to him. She did and she was amused at what he did with the number. He smiled at the woman to acknowledge the fact that he received it, but on the way out of the restaurant he threw the napkin in the garbage without a second thought.

"So when are you getting back on the dating scene?" Tahara asked him. She had volunteered on more than one occasion to let his son stay over while he went out on a date. He never took her up on it though.

"I'm not into all of that."

"How are you going to find the woman of your dreams? You can't find her while sitting over here watching movies with me and listening to me whining about my day." She rambled on and on, not really paying attention to the look on his face.

"Do you think I spend too much time here?"

"Yes,"

"Am I getting on your nerves or cramping your style?"

"No, of course not. I meant that you might miss your future wife by sitting deep up in the house with me. You know I'm a recluse. I don't want it to rub off on you," she said as she rubbed his thigh slightly. He felt that familiar pressure returning.

"Guess what?"

"What?" She looked at him waiting for him to speak.

"I have already found the woman I want to be my future wife." His smile was bright and his dimples deepened as Tahara saw the light in his eyes. She didn't know why her heart constricted like it did. It wasn't as if they were even remotely close to being anything more than friends.

"That's great news! When did you propose?" She tried to be excited for him, but she couldn't. Even though he had no idea of her feelings for him, she felt crushed all the same.

"Oh I haven't proposed yet. In fact, she doesn't even know how I feel," he admitted to her while twirling his glass between his fingers.

She was stunned, "She doesn't know? Aren't you nervous that she might say no?" Even though she could not imagine any woman in her right mind saying no to Mike.

"Of course I am, but the man chooses the wife and I chose her. I just need to convince her that I'm the man of her dreams, the man that can quench each and every one of her desires," he informed her.

"Well, okay then! That's some deep stuff right there." She wished she could one day find a man to say those words to her, to make her feel loved and adored. She guessed it was not meant to be for her. It had been so long since she'd felt a man's touch that she hardly remembered what it felt like.

"I know. I'm madly in love with her. I think she is the most beautiful woman in this entire world. Her strength amazes me. The love and dedication she has for her family is ...." He shook his head without completing the sentence.

"Wow, you love her that much that she makes you speechless."

"Yes, I do." He told her. She looked into his eyes and saw a flash of something, but before she could determine the meaning, it was gone.

***

"Mom, can we have a snack?" Tahara's son Kyle asked as he entered the living room followed by Mike's son Dylan. They stopped short when they saw Mike stilling on the sofa.

"Dad, what are you doing here? I thought you were going out with Uncle Lou?" Dylan asked his dad. For two teenage boys, they were very perceptive where their parents were concerned. They had each suggested that they needed to go out and have fun instead of always staying home.

"I changed my mind at the last minute."

"Awww man, does that mean I have to go home? Me and Kyle just got to the hard level." His face had fallen with the thought of leaving.

"No, you don't have to leave. In fact, I'm going to hang out here for a while and watch some movies with Tahara." he informed the boys. They both yelled in excitement as they made their way to the kitchen to raid the fridge.

"You know I'm going to have to buy you groceries one day," Mike said to her.

"What for?" She was confused by what he said.

"I know my boy eats like there is no tomorrow. He is

like a bottomless pit." He shook his head thinking about the way the boys ate.

"Oh that's no problem. I know my son does the same at your house, so it's even."

"Yeah, but my boy is over here a whole lot more than yours is at my house. As a matter of fact, we both are over here a lot." She thought about what he said. It was true. They did see a lot of one another. They even communicated on the phone and computer. There was hardly a day that went by that they didn't have some sort of exchange.

"It's all good. What are friends for?" That was his thought exactly. What are friends for? Immediately he knew what it was he needed to do.

***

It had been a few days since Mike hung out with her. He hadn't called or texted her or anything. She was wondering if she had done something to upset him. Maybe he was really busy with work she thought to herself. She was going to be off of work for the next two weeks. Even though the time off work was needed, it wasn't wanted because it was going to send her further in debt.

She picked up the phone, took a deep breath and prepared to beg the rep to let her make some sort of arrangement for her utility bill. Once she was connected to a live person, she went into the spiel that she had practiced. Before she could finish, the rep interrupted her, "I'm sorry Ms. Jones but my computer is showing that you have a zero balance."

Tahara thought she was hearing things, "Excuse me, what did you just say?"

"Your balance is zero. Someone made a payment on your bill yesterday and it covered the whole account," the woman on the phone informed her.

"Are you sure?" She couldn't believe what she was hearing. Someone had paid her $500.00 utility bill. That was not a small amount of money.

"Yes ma'am. I'm positive."

"Can you tell me who paid it?" She would have to thank whoever had done it in a major way.

"No ma'am, I can't. They wanted to remain anonymous."

"Oh my goodness, I can't believe this! Thank you so much and have a lovely Christmas," she told the lady.

The woman's voice shared Tahara's excitement, "You too dear and enjoy your holidays also." She hung up the phone and danced around the living room. She was going to have money to at least get her babies a few gifts for Christmas after all. She dropped to her knees and said a prayer for the blessing she had just received.

When she told her kids about the good fortune, they danced around the room and hugged one another. That was the best gift ever.

The next day, she was cleaning the house when she heard her phone ringing. Once she got to it, she noticed that it was Mike.

"Hey Mike, what's up?" she asked him. She was happy to finally be hearing from him.

"Nothing much, what do you have going on right now?" he asked.

"I'm doing a little cleaning. Why, what's up?" she was curious now.

"I need you to go shopping with me. I have quite a few gifts to get and I need a woman's opinion. What do you say? Can you help me out?" He pleaded with her.

"Yeah sure, I can do that." She was in a good mood.

Shopping with her friend could only improve that mood.
***

She was amazed at all of the items they had in the carts. He had so much stuff that she had to get a cart to help him out.

"Wow Mike, this is a lot of toys," she told him.

"Yeah, I know. You remember me telling you about my future wife, right?" He looked in her direction and waited for her to confirm remembering.

"Yes, I do."

"Well she has kids and I want to do something nice for them. You know, since I'm going to be their step father and all."

"You are serious aren't you?"

"Yes, I told you that I was."

"I know, but I didn't think it was like this. I mean, wow, when can I meet this woman that has captured your heart like this?" She needed to see what kind of woman it took to make a man like Mike desire her in such a way.

"Sure you can. How about on Christmas Eve? How about if we all spend it together? You know, bring it in together, drinking egg nog and maybe going to church. What do you say?" She saw the excitement in his eyes as he spoke. She really didn't want to spend her holidays watching him and his lady all in love but she could see that it would mean a lot to him.

"Okay, that's fine. The more the merrier." she said knowing that it was possible she would end up feeling like a third wheel. But she knew that she had to be there for her friend.

On the way back to her house, she told him about the mystery person paying her bill and he was excited for her.

She told him that was why she bought the toys to donate, to sort of "pay it forward". After a few minutes, she had a sneaking suspicion that he was the one that paid it but she didn't ask him though.

***

Tahara cooked up a storm for Christmas. Usually it was only her and her children. This year she had guests coming over. It was around seven that evening when Mike finally arrived with a truck full of gifts. The boys helped him bring everything in while Tahara looked on.

Mike walked over to her and gave her a hug. "Ummmm...you smell delicious," he said as he put his nose to her neck and inhaled deeply. He felt her stiffen in his arms and knew he should cool it.

"Thanks, I was making a cake and other goodies." She smiled at him while trying to calm her nerves. His touch had done something to her. He could tell that her body was on fire from that simple act of him smelling her.

"I hope you have some chocolate in there somewhere." His eyes begged her.

She laughed at him and his sweet tooth. "Only for you, I have a chocolate cake only for you."

His heart swelled with love for this woman. He knew that she was meant for him and only him, "I can't wait to sample it," he told her. Tahara didn't know why but she got the feeling he was talking about more than the cake. That couldn't be possible because he had his future wife and her children coming over to spend the holiday with them.

"Come on and we will get you that sample." He followed her to the kitchen while his eyes took in the swaying of her ample bottom. He had to get a handle on things before he messed up his plan.

He sat in the kitchen with her while she finished up the food. He listened to her talk and let her voice comfort him. That was why he had fallen head over heels in love with her, because of her heart and her spirit. He was sure that he was doing the right thing, making the right choice.

***

As the night progressed, they sat around and enjoyed their time together with them all watching Christmas movies and singing holiday songs. He knew that this was what he wanted as he took in the whole scene. They were all happy and they made a lovely team.

The kids all wanted to open gifts that night. Tahara and Mike suggested that they wait until the morning time. Tahara asked him about the arrival of his lady friend and he brushed her off by saying she would be there later. He knew she was wondering if something had happened to their plans.

At twelve on the dot, Mike stood up and passed out a gift to each person.

"I thought you said to wait?" Tahara asked him while smiling. She was excited to see that he handed her a gift, he could see it in her eyes.

"One present isn't going to hurt. After that you guys will have to wait to open the rest." The kids agreed because they were excited to be opening at least one.

They each took turns opening their gifts with Lisa, Tahara's six year old daughter, going first. Mike had gotten her a Barbie dollhouse that she had been asking about forever. Then came the boys, he had gotten each one a tablet, to their delight. Tahara looked at him.

"You sneak you got me to pick those things out." She said.

He laughed out loud, "Guilty. I needed some sort of idea."

"So, what did you get me? I don't think I gave you an idea for that."

His smile faded. "Why don't you open it and find out?" he insisted.

"Wait, how about you open yours first?" she suggested to him.

He tore into his present and a big smile lit up his face when he saw the gift. It was a large portrait of them all at a picnic together last summer. The picture was his favorite by far.

"I love it!" he exclaimed while still inspecting it.

"I'm glad you do. Where will you put it since you are soon to be married?" She covered her mouth quickly. She had forgotten the kids were in hearing distance.

"Married? Dad, you are getting married?" Dylan asked him. The room was silent. Everyone was waiting on Mike's response. He didn't respond to his son.

***

Mike looked at Tahara.

"Open your gift." He said. His look made her nervous. The room was quiet as she ripped the paper off and opened the box. Inside that box was a smaller black box. Her heart was thumping in her chest as she pulled out the black box. She opened it slowly and gasped. Inside the box was a gorgeous 2 carat diamond ring. The ring that she always looked at when she went to the jewelry store. The ring that he convinced her to try on when he went to pick up his watch, her dream ring!

He took the box from her hand and got down on one knee. She felt the tears stinging her eyes.

"Tahara, my beautiful Tahara, I love you oh so much. I

love the way you smile, the way you talk, the way you care, the way you love, the way you do everything. You are my light on a dark day. You are my best friend. I can talk to you about anything. I never get tired of being around you and when I'm not, I wonder what you are doing. I want to be with you, to spend my life showing you what real love is. Let me love you and make you whole again. Can we be a family? Will you marry me, baby?" His eyes were moist as he took the ring from the box and slid it on her finger. The kids stood around waiting for her reply.

"I don't know what to say," she mumbled while trying to keep from crying.

"Say yes." She heard the kids scream and she laughed.

"Yes," she said as she looked in his eyes. He stood up and pulled her into his arms and held on to her for dear life. He leaned down and captured her lips in their first of many kisses to come. Her heart felt complete and happy.

Tahara's toes curled at the way his kiss made her feel. She couldn't believe it! He loved her and he had chosen her for his wife.

After the kiss ended he looked down at her, "I'd like to introduce you to my very soon to be wife, Tahara."

She blushed at the thought and caressed his cheek. "I love you, Mike."

"I love you too, baby." he whispered in her ear while she was thinking that this was the best Christmas gift she had ever received.

THE END
2013 Shemeka Mitchell

He Sees You When You're Sleeping
By
D C Rogers

For all those girls and boys who get their toys on Christmas day. They are the lucky good ones. You sicken Poor Anti with your sweetness. Even the bad ones, the ones who get nothing but a lump of coal. Somehow they're worse as they're just one more step away from meeting him. He's not a big jolly creature like his metaphorical brother. No he's thin and twisted by evil. Strange how evil can warp and twist a creature like that.

That old tune people sing. He sees you while you're sleeping. You wouldn't think something so sinister would be about his jolly old brother now?

It's not. It's about the Anti-Claus and he hates you vile little creatures. He comes for you, the truly bad evil children. The nasty ones, who pull the legs of insects then leave them there suffering. Oh you little devils you're the ones that make him smile, why you ask?

You're the perfect specimens who make the best targets for teaching a lesson that you will never forget. Unfortunately some turn away from evil through what he does. Those saps he spits upon. Some go completely mad because of what he does. Then once in a blue moon he really manages to create a truly viscous individual. Today, for the first time, you're going learn how.

***

"Johnny, oh Johnny come in son. It's nearly bed time, tomorrow is Christmas day!" shouted Johnny Herman's step mother. The small boy had chipped a small hole in the ice of his father's pond, where he was trying to poke the trapped and expensive fish beneath with a sharp stick.

Anti-Claus viewed all this from the safety of a snow covered lamppost, how? He could go invisible like his goody two shoes counterpart. This truly repulsive specimen of a child was his first victim for tonight. Little Johnny was a terror to his folks and bane to his small sister. He was going to find a special present under his bed later tonight.

Clapping his hands in anticipation he flew off the lamp in search of his second quarry. The evil being had only two targets in this area that deserved the Anti-Claus treatment. Besides if he did too many at any one time his goody-two-shoes brother would realise and then try to stop him.

There she was, his second target. Anti-Claus landed quietly upon her window sill and peered in at little Sally Jenkins. She sat there, with her dolls and teddies, playing at some kind of tea party. However, this tea party had something glaringly wrong with it and he found it so amusingly macabre. All her toys were sat there in a circle. All their heads were missing , leaving either blank rubber stumps or frayed cotton wool filled holes. This girl would seem at first certifiable until you learnt she knew exactly what she was doing; it was all in order to annoy her poor single mum. The poor mother who cried herself to sleep because her daughter destroys everything in her life, from presents bought to new relationships.

Something quite important will come to an end tonight for your mummy, Anti Claus thought. Especially when you find the extra special present I hid under your bed Jane. He left the little girl to her devices. Flying off, he sought out little Johnny's abode again.

The evil little boy was sneaking upstairs to his little

sister's room. He hated that his parents loved her more. She always got better presents and more of them than him at Christmas or her birthday. He was going make her pay lots for being his parent's favourite. Especially now it was the day before the big day. Anti-Claus loved this as Johnny genuinely was a product of bad parenting.

The father had remarried and then, with the new Mrs Herman, had fathered a little girl. It was all a case of favouritism. Anti clapped his hands with glee, it was the most wonderful time of year after all. The evil Claus floated unseen by the window of Johnny's sister's room. The little girl was sat there playing with her dollies. None decapitated, how horribly cute. Anti-Claus was almost sick at the sweetness. Johnny entered the room with a truly evil look upon his little eight year old face.

Sam his four year old sister looked up in terror.

"Oh no Johnny please don't."

"Don't be a sissy I haven't even done anything yet you big baby." She knew what was coming though.

"You have that look on your face Johnny, please I love you." Anti-Claus screwed up his face in disgust. Then silently cursed as he had seen a small flicker of emotion in Johnny's eyes.

"Well I don't love you, you spoiled brat," He shouted, before grabbing the small girl by her long golden locks. He laughed as he dragged her about the room by her hair. Anti-Claus clapped to see such joy but his work was far from done. This was the distraction he needed to perform his trick.

Floating from the girl's bedroom to Johnny's room he clicked his fingers making the window swing open. He floated in and could hear the young girl's screams as he went about his work. Anti-Claus even started to hum a little tune.

***
"Slay bells ring, you're not listening."
"In the lane, blood is glistening."
"It's a frightful sight."
"We're dying tonight."
"Running from a winter Terror-land."
***

He even did a little butt wiggle as he danced over to the boy's bed. The sounds of pain and anguish coming from the other room made him all the happier. Anti-Claus clicked his fingers once more and a box of matches appeared in his hand. Laughing to himself, he placed the box of matches under Johnny's bed. He loved setting these things up.

"Johnny what are you doing to your sister!" Came a shout from down the landing.

"He's pulling my hair mummy," Cried the little girl. What a wimp she was.

"Apologise to your sister and then get to your bedroom you naughty boy."

"Shut up, you're not my mother."

"You'll be lucky to have anything for Christmas tomorrow Johnny." Despite his back chat, Anti-Claus heard the kid begin to make his way across the landing to his room. He quickly flew out the window and, with a click of his magical fingers, it silently closed behind him.

Johnny walked into his room and felt a strange draft blow over him. Anti-Claus gently floated down to the kitchen window where both Johnny's parents were arguing; Sam stood in their midst.

"He's a god damn terror Phillip," Johnny's step-mother said, stroking Sammy's hurt head.

"I agree," Johnny's Father said, "he's taken this jealousy thing to far. I fear this will be his last Christmas with us as a family."

"I hope it's not me influencing you. I wouldn't want you to get rid of your son for me," Sam cried. "I don't want Johnny to go. Deep down, I know he's nice daddy." she began to wail. Claus hated the crying but loved the parents; they were digging their own graves.

"Job done here," he laughed to himself, "now to set up the last one in this place!"

"We know darling but he might hurt you bad next time," the father said and Claus clapped with joy at the families' misfortune. He slowly ascended into the air and, for the time being, happy at how things were going with his first victims. It was time to set up the little girl's fate. As he flew, he tried to think of a good easy way to exact his brand of evil against her family.

Anti-Claus soon descended upon the house of Sally Jenkins. He was drawn to the kitchen. The sounds of sobbing were like catnip to him. He viewed through the window and, inside, Sally's mother sobbed into her hands.

She picked up the house phone and dialled for that new guy she met down the bar last month. They had been on a few dates and she didn't want to be alone for Christmas.

"Hello is that Jeff? Hi it's Nancy. Listen you said you didn't have plans for Christmas would you like to come over here tonight? Maybe stay for Christmas dinner?" Unknown to her mother little Sally was sat upon the stairs, listening intently.

She didn't like Jeff, he took her mummy away from her. She would have to make both mummy and Jeff pay for hurting her feelings like that. With delight upon his soul, the Anti-Claus made his way to Sally's bedroom. He entered by way of his usual tricks. As he floated there, trying to decide on the best tool for the job, he tapped his lip and sang a new little jingle.

***

"I watch you when you're sleeping."
"I watch when you're awake."
"I know if you've been good or bad."
"So don't be good for goodness sake!"

***

As inspiration hit him, he clicked his fingers and a large, sharp knife materialised under the girl's bed. With his evil fun now set up for the night, Anti Claus drifted out of the window. He would find a place where he would wait until night came and when the two children would discover the dangerous new toys he had left under their beds. He sat unseen, above the rabble, on the marble statue of some person who had died hundreds of years ago. They made him sick to his stomach as they ran from shop to shop looking for last minute gifts for their loved ones. Still, some of it gave him glee. Such as, when they came out empty handed. Sad expressions because they could not get the game little Billy wanted or the perfume some mistress had required for their elicit, Christmas fling.

It was nearly time to view his handy work when something else caught his attention. A man looking manic had entered a jewellers shop. Anti-Claus knew the look all too well, he also knew the man to be Barry Gardner. He was one such down and out that he had dealt with on his seventh Christmas. His had been a particularly nasty case. The lake had frozen over that year, to the point where skating was being allowed. His sisters were going on Christmas day to skate there. Barry had hated them so much, so that Anti-Claus had left a strong lump hammer for him.

The little boy had spent a good few hours that night weakening the ice with his new hammer. In the morning his sisters had gone out onto the lake to skate. The ice cracked under their weight and, unfortunately, they both drowned. Barry's dad had left and his mother went mad with grief. He never got found out but he knew it was his fault and still harboured that grief, which seemed to had made its decision to finally manifest. Attempting to feed a drugs habit, he held up the jewellery shop. The staff were as helpful as ever yet fearful for their own lives. They filled his bag up with goodies, while repeatedly pressing the silent alarm under the desk. It informed the police, who just happened to be waiting in the parking lot, that there was an armed robbery in progress. Barry didn't make it out of the mall, well not standing at least. It was also found that the gun he had used was just a plastic toy. With that bit of fun over, Claus took the skies once more.

Something suddenly frightened him. It the only sound in the world that sent shivers up his spine: jingling bells. Somewhere up above, the jolly, fat, red-clad man was riding his sleigh, ready to dispense presents to all the foul, good little children. Anti-Claus had to hide from him, lest his plans be ruined for this year.

A few minutes later, when he sensed all was well again, Anti-Claus glided off. Floating a good few feet above the town, Anti-Claus could see both houses.

Not that it mattered to him. He could after all project his sight anywhere he wanted; it just left his physical form somewhat unguarded. Now that the jolly red one had done his rounds, he was free to do this as soon as the suggestions had taken root.

"Look under your bed there's mischief to be had," Anti whispered into his balled hands. He opened his palms that now homed two smoke filled bubbles. A gentle blow from his pursed lips sent them floating off into the night air. Away to do their damage, Anti-Claus just floated waiting.

Little Johnny lay fitfully in bed. He hated it. He did love his little sister deep down, he just hated that his parents doted more on her than him. As he lay there, a small smoke bubble, invisible to his eyes, floated up to his ear. Once there it popped releasing its words.

"Johnny your parents always buy more presents for Sammy every year. Wouldn't it pay them back if you destroyed all her presents this Christmas? Well then, look under your bed and you will find the present I left you to help you do just that."

"I think that's a wonderful idea," he said as he flopped his head over the side of the bed. There in front of him lay something that he was told never to play with, matches! Fearful yet full of vigour, only a nasty boy could muster over the thought of destroying his little sister's toys. He slowly reached for the box of forbidden items until his hand wrapped around them.

Anti-Claus projected his sight and watched Johnny leave his bedroom. He was ready to exact his revenge on both Sammy and his parents. He knew exactly what to do. His parents had said that the presents would be under the tree. He'd set fire to their presents so only he alone would have something to open in the morning.

He knelt next to the presents and opened the forbidden box. Then, taking three matches at once, he struck them on the side. The fire flared up on the small wooden stick startling the small child with both the heat and brightness. He dropped the matches upon the carpet where the pile quickly burst into flames. Johnny watched wide eyed as the fire quickly spread to the presents, eating them up before spreading towards the Christmas tree. Anti-Claus laughed and clapped his hands at the chaos.

The dry, real wooden tree also caught fire quickly. Johnny was scared, he didn't know what to do. He went to get up. He had to warn his parents but, as he turned around, the fire had already spread towards the stairs. He screamed, he didn't know what to do next.

Johnny did the only thing he could do. He ran outside, screaming for help, hoping to wake his neighbours. His parents hadn't noticed the blaze yet. Smoke was even coming through some of the windows upstairs already. Johnny got the neighbours attention over the spectacle of his blazing house but all they could do was scream. Johnny turned back to the house, only to see a shape like his father emerge from the doorway. He was ablaze and carrying a small burning shape in his arms. Johnny knew, in mind boggling terror. that it was his sister.

The blazing form of his father fell to its knee, screaming. Johnny's sanity left him as he watched the life leave his father's body. From that day on Johnny would never speak to any living soul again and just spend the rest of his life staring in horror as the memories haunted his soul.

For Anti-Claus the whole of Johnny's life was mapped out for him to see. Not totally satisfied with the way Johnny would turn out but happy with the carnage he had caused. He closed his eyes and moved his consciousness to his next victim's location. The smoky thought bubble he had sent was just reaching little Sally as he watched; It popped right by her ear.

"Sally. Hello darling," the bubbled voice said and caused little girl to moan in her sleep. "Nasty mummy has invited that new horrible man for Christmas." Sally opened her eyes.

"Nasty mummy, she's mine not his," she quietly said.

"There's something under your bed, use it to show how

much you love your mummy." Somewhere far above the town, Anti-Claus smiled evilly. The little girl, now fully awake, leapt from her bed. She scooted down to take a look for her 'gift'. There under the bed a large chef's knife glinted. Its edge was ethereally sharp with an electric blue sheen in the dim light.

Downstairs, Sally's mum's boyfriend watched late night Christmas Eve telly. He laughed at some comedy on an obscure channel. It was the first time he had felt happy for a while, Sally's mum made him feel wanted even if the little girl was a bit odd. Her mum had gone to bed an hour or so earlier.

He didn't hear as Sally stealthily sneaked through the darkened room. He did notice with wide terrified eyes as the girl leapt up on the sofa next to him.

"Holy shit Sally," he shouted and then looked at the glinting steel in her hands.

"Mummy is mine, NOT yours." He didn't manage to get a reply out as his throat suddenly opened wide. Sally revelled in the red waterfall that fell from the hated man's sliced windpipe as he choked his life away.

An hour of work later Sally's mum was woken from her slumber by small hands tugging at her.

"Mummy, mummy. I have an extra special Christmas surprise for you."

"Sally, what do you mean?" she was groggy from lack of sleep.

"Just follow me ok." She did as she was told. Her daughter led her across their landing then down the stairs. The dining room was lit by the eerie glow of tea lights. This made Sally's mum cross, her little girl had been using matches or a lighter. All this fled from her already fragile mind as she took in the terrible sight before her.

Sat in five of the four chairs were some of the girl's larger teddies. Their heads had been removed and stuffing popped of the holes. They were sat at the table which hosted the most macabre meal she had ever seen. The man who had treated her so nicely was now sat lifeless and headless at the far end of the table. His severed head had been positioned on a plate so that its dead eyes could stare at the horrific scene in front of it. Her mind couldn't take anymore and finally snapped. Sally's mother crumpled into a foetal position at her daughter's feet while Sally just smiled on at her handy work.

Anti-Claus grinned once more as he could see the girl's future mapped out. Sally would go into counselling but it would be totally ineffective. However, the doctors wouldn't suspect a thing, the clever little girl would fool them all. Sally would be set free five years later and this small town would lay witness to its very first serial killer in its history.

Happy with his work for this year Anti-Claus floated ever higher into the sky. With a quick click of his fingers he vanished into snowflakes just as a fresh batch started to fall from the winter night's sky. It would be a white Christmas this year, bringing joy to many families bar two.

Remember the Anti-Claus because, if you know child who is that terrible, it could be your town he visits next year!

THE END
2013 D.C Rogers

Peter's Wish
By
William O'Brien

In a serene and clammy room
A tree did sit in festive gloom
With no snow, tinsel or elves
Caramel biscuits high up on shelves

One boy home, nurturing the cold
Enters a man bearded and old
Why are you sitting in the dark?
Angels whisper, jumping quarks

Room all alight, glitters and twinkles
Candles, halos, icicles that jingle
Did you look for the hidden present?
No, he replied looking to heaven

Hmmm… said Santa, scratching his beard
Waved his hand, a dozen elves appeared
Climbing they played with baubles of gold
Snow started falling a secret told

Under the tree, a box gave a truth
Sending a message for future youth
Gift of knowing, guardians would tell
Wish was given, the coin in the well

***

© 2013 William O'Brien

A Dead Medium Spin-Off
The Spirits Of Christmas
By
Peter John

Barbara Smith dropped the four shopping bags onto the kitchen table and watched as the colour slowly returned to her fingers. Christmas was fast approaching and she had many more shopping trips to get through before she would have everything that she needed for that one solitary day of the year. It's only one day, she thought. One day but it took half a year to prepare for it. There were lists to write, presents to buy, cards to post and sugary or fattening food to stock up with. It had always puzzled Barbara why people, and she included herself in this, spent the whole year checking how many calories are in this, and how much saturated whatever is in that, but come Christmas they're all out there buying goose fat by the jar full. The obvious reason was that it was tradition but Barbara saw that as a rather poor excuse for watching your weight for twelve months only to put on two stone in two days. Every year she seriously considered serving up fresh salad and a low calorie pasta dish on the big day but every year she still ended up buying the same traditional fare, a turkey the size of a highland terrier, that just barely fitted into her oven, and a waist-high sack of potatoes. It just wouldn't be Christmas without a fat golden bird and all the trimmings. It was the same every year but this year something was fundamentally different; this was the first Christmas that Barbara would be spending in the company of the dead.

It must have been about three months ago now, Barbara mused, it's gone rather quickly in fact. Three months had passed since she had inherited the gift of sight from a woman who, in the space of one week, she had grown to respect after spending two decades thinking of her as a miserable, old crone. May Elizabeth Trump was the last person she would have ever thought she would miss but each time she thought of her she felt her eyes begin to well up. I had always ridiculed Margaret for being May's one and only friend, Barbara thought. She had been right all along, Margaret saw May's hidden capacity for compassion from day one, where all I saw was a grumpy old woman who would shout the odds at you should you ever step an inch out of line. That was all before she died of course. May's death had been the making of her, Barbara had decided. May's death had shown her all the things she had been searching for her whole life. It was only after May's spirit had announced itself to them that she had realised just how wasted her life had been. All those dark creepy nights spent poking about in old houses or playing around with macabre picture cards, all in the belief that she had some kind of psychic power that would allow her to see past the grave. All those years of treating a drafty window as a cold spot or the sound of a scurrying mouse as the whispers of earth-bound souls. May was her first real spectral encounter and, after 68 years of envisioning the moment, it hadn't been quite how she had imagined it. Not that it really mattered in the end. Something had rubbed off on her and, whether it was a gift from May or just her own psychic ability finally kicking into gear, Barbara had started to see ghosts on a regular basis not long after. In fact, nowadays she saw more of the dead than she did of the living, especially as they had the knack of appearing at the most inconvenient moments. Once the word had got out that Barbara could see them, all the local spirits had descended on her with one hundred and one different requests. A lot of it was about contacting their surviving relatives, or even ancestors, as some of the dead folk had been around quite a while, but there were a few who just seemed to like the company of the living. There were three such sprits huddled by Barbara's kitchen sink as she walked over to her kettle.

"What's in the bags, Madam Smith?" Gerald asked as he pointed a bony finger towards the kitchen table. His voice was nasal and had a hollow, whistle-like quality that made him sound as if he were speaking through panpipes. Gerald had started to hang around Barbara about two months ago. He was 6 foot tall and about 2 foot wide, by Barbara's reckoning, and he was dressed in a two-piece black suit that draped off him as if he were no more than a coat hanger. Barbara had the suspicion that he had lost a lot of weight just before he had died but he refused to confirm it. Gerald didn't like talking about his death, Barbara had very quickly discovered. He had a habit of suddenly walking off through the nearest wall whenever Barbara had broached the subject, which she found to be a very effective conversation stopper. Yes it was pretty rude behaviour, even for a dead man, but Barbara often used it to her own advantage. Gerald always spoke in short blunt sentences and his tone was generally sober even with the whistle. He tended to question everything but he never seemed to actually listen to the answers people gave him. Barbara could very quickly lose her patience with him, which was usually when she would start asking him about his death knowing that it would compel him to leave.

"What business is it of yours?" Barbara replied with a sharp tone, as she shook the kettle to check if it had enough water in it and then switched it on.

"There's no need to get defensive, Madam Smith," Brian

said through his semi-permanent smile, "he was just asking." Brian had started to darken her door a couple of weeks before Gerald had appeared. The two ghosts were like chalk and cheese in both appearance and personality. Brian was no more than 5 foot tall and had a wide, circular stomach. His multi-coloured sweater with its thick vertical stripes made him look like an over-inflated beach ball with legs. Barbara quite liked his company, on most days he was usually rather chipper and he had an infectious smile.

"He's always asking something or other. That's the whole problem, you know that!" Barbara heaped a spoonful of coffee granules into her favourite mug and then turned towards the fridge.

"Have you got an issue with that?" Gerald said.

"On most days, yes I have, Gerald." Barbara pulled open the fridge door and took out a half full bottle of milk. She raised the bottle up to her nose and took a deep sniff before bringing it to her coffee mug.

"What is in those bags then, Madam Smith?" The voice was as quiet as the squeak of a less than boisterous mouse. It had a timid, shaky quality, as if the issuer suffered from perpetual anxiety.

"It's just some Christmas shopping Martha, that's all," Barbara replied. She couldn't see the nervous ghost. She's probably hiding behind Brian, she thought.

"Christmas! Christmas shopping you say," Brian was still smiling but there was a hint of sarcasm in his voice. "I didn't think you were into that old rubbish, Madam Smith."

"Is it that time again? God help us!" Gerald announced, his whistle seemed to hit a slightly higher pitch than usual.

"I don't like Christmas," Martha squeaked, "all that noise makes me nervous."

"Everything makes you nervous Martha," Brian pointed

out.

"I know," Martha sighed, "but at Christmas time I get even worse. It's all the noise and hullabaloo that goes with it. The shrill cries of excited children, all that doorstep singing business and the bangers always give me an awful fright."

"Bangers, Martha? Don't you mean Christmas crackers?" Barbara asked as she poured hot water into her coffee mug.

"Do they go bang, Madam Smith?"

"Yes, I guess they do."

"Then they're bangers in my book and they'd make me jump clean out of my skin if I still had any."

"What's the point of Christmas anyway?" Gerald whistled.

"Beats me," Brain shrugged. "I remember celebrating it back when I was alive and it all seemed like too much hard work for very little gain, even back then. All that messing about and wasted money just for one day. You get up too early in the morning, still half cut from the few celebration tipples you drank the night before, and then spend the day feeling like death warmed up. You open a few presents, which are usually nothing more than a few pairs of socks and a satsuma, and then you have to stick your arm up a turkey's backside and drag out its innards."

"It can be hard work, I grant you that," Barbara said, as she leant against the kitchen side and sipped her coffee.

"I can handle hard work," Brian said. "Christmas isn't hard work, Madam Smith, it's tiresome is what it is. In my experience, hard work usually leaves you in profit at the end of the day. A day's pay for a day's work and all that; I don't see any profit in Christmas!"

"What about spending time with your family, you must

have enjoyed that?"

"What, that bunch of freeloaders?" Gerald said.

"Too right Gerry," Brian agreed. "Like vultures around a carcass they were, if memory serves."

"I was always nervous around large groups of people," Martha added.

"What, even your family?" Barbara asked.

"I think so, I don't recall a time when I wasn't nervous, to tell the truth."

"You're better off not remembering if you ask me," Brain said, managing to sound grumpy and regretful even though his smile refused to break. "Whenever I think back, all I can remember is hardship and disappointment."

"I can't think of anything good about Christmas," Gerald said and Barbara suddenly realised that is was the first time she had heard him say anything that wasn't in the form of a question.

"Can you?" Gerald suddenly added and then Barbara sighed.

"I can't believe that none of you have any happy memories of Christmas," she said. "I have nothing but fond memories of this time of year. Yes it can be tough and yes sometimes we all don't get on as well as we should but that all pales into insignificance when you look into the children's eyes as they find out that Santa Claus has been and filled their stockings. Christmas is a wonderful time and, even though I dread all the preparation, every year it always seems worthwhile on the day. It fills my heart and it always gives me a positive start to the new year."

"What absolute rubbish! Madam Smith, I had always thought of you as a woman of stability not a gooey eyed school girl." Brian's smile drooped for a fraction of a second but sprang straight back into its usual upward curl.

"Don't you remember when you were a child and excitedly waiting to hear the sound of sleigh bells?"

"Nope," Brian replied.

"No, not really," Martha squeaked.

"Should I?" Gerald whistled. Barbara sighed again and then took a long, slow slurp of coffee. This wouldn't do, she thought, as she put her empty mug onto the kitchen side. She looked over at the sink and saw the plug hanging by its little silvery chain.

"I don't know if this will actually work on a ghost but I would like to try," she said as she picked up the black, plastic sink plug and unhooked the other end of the chain.

"Try what?" Gerald asked.

"I want to see if I can regress you through hypnosis and see if I can bring back those festive, childhood memories."

"I don't know if that's such a good idea, Madam Smith," Brain said.

"What if they're bad memories?" Gerald said or asked, Barbara wasn't certain which.

"We will find that out, won't we," Barbara commanded more than said. She took a couple of steps into the middle of the kitchen and dangled the sink plug in front of the three ghosts.

"I take it that you've done this before Madam Smith," Brian said.

"Of course I have!"

"And it works does it?"

"Most of the time yes, well quite often at any rate."

"Is it dangerous?" Gerald asked and Barbara was sure it was a proper question this time.

"I doubt it."

"So you're not actually sure," Brian pointed out.

"You're dead already, what harm can it do to you now?"

"She's got a point," Martha piped up and Barbara could sense a little more confidence in her voice than she was used to.

"Can you see the plug, Martha?" Barbara asked, she tried to peer around Brian's large frame but still couldn't catch a glimpse of the anxious spirit.

"Yes I can, madam Smith," Martha replied. Her voice had regained its trademark squeak.

"OK, are you all ready?"

"Ready for what?" Gerald said and Barbara took it as a yes. She started to swing the sink plug gently to and fro.

"Keep your eyes on the plug," she said in low, whispery voice. The two ghosts that she could see followed the sink plug as it swung from side to side, Barbara hoped that Martha was doing the same.

"You are feeling sleepy."

"No I'm not!"

"Please take this seriously Brian!"

"But I'm dead, I can't sleep. If I do I just transcend dimensions, I thought you knew that about us." Barbara had to admit that he had a point.

"OK, just shut up and concentrate on the plug then!" Barbara continued to swing the sink plug.

"Are you concentrating, Martha?"

"Yes Mummy," her voice was still squeaky but there was no fear or anxiety in it.

"Where are you, Martha?" Barbara said.

"I'm tucked up in bed, I'm waiting for Santa Claus," Martha said in an excited voice.

"I think it's worked on Martha, don't you Brian?"

"Be quiet, stop talking. If Santa knows we're awake he won't leave any presents!" Brian whispered in the high-pitched , clucky tone of a young boy. "He's bringing me a bike this year for sure. It's going to be a bright red one, just like the one in the toy shop window, now be quiet or he'll never come." This is working better than I thought it would, Barbara surmised. It's usually pretty hit and miss when I try this on living folk.

"Are you alright there, Gerald?"

"Oh I will be soon enough," Gerald's voice sounded lighter, less of a drone, and his whistle wasn't as prominent. "One hour to go before my shift ends and I rush off home and climb into my Santa suit. The kids will be so excited, it's been a good year and we've managed to get some cracking presents for them. I can't wait to see little Billy's face when he unwraps that train set, he's been ogling it through the toy shop window for months. This is going to be the best Christmas ever!" Gerald was smiling. Barbara couldn't believe it, an actual smile. She had always thought that his face would crumble like a rockslide if he were ever to curl his mouth in such a way.

"Right then, the night has passed and it's now early on Christmas morning," Barbara said. All three ghosts let out wide yawns and stretched their arms.

"Where are you, Martha?"

"He's been," Martha cried out. "Santa's been and look at how full my stocking is, it's fit to burst!"

"Oh no!" Brian said, "I must have dosed off and missed him again." "What have you got there Billy? Wow, that's a mighty fine train set," Gerald's eyes glistened brightly as he spoke. He stretched out his thin, bony arms as if expecting an embrace.

"A bicycle," Brian cried, "I've got a bicycle. It's red and it's bright and it's so shiny, I bet it's as fast as a rocket ship as well. This is just the best Christmas ever!"

"Mummy, Mummy, Mummy. Santa's been and look, he's

even eaten one of those mince pies we made." Barbara still couldn't see Martha but there seemed to be a faint glow coming from behind Brian. Gerald closed his arms around something unseen and a single tear escaped his eye. Barbara decided that enough was enough and clicked her fingers.

"Awake!" She commanded. Brian was the first to react. He took an involuntary step backwards and his wide, unblinking eyes darted around the room. His infectious grin flat lined across his face and he looked like he had just been abruptly awoken from a sleep that he hadn't realised he was having, which wasn't so far from the truth. Gerald casually wiped the tear from his eye and then started to clap his hands together. He was still smiling.

"Was that an enlightening experience?" Gerald said as he tapered off his applause. A small glowing form floated out from behind Brian. About four foot tall and hovering a foot above the floor, Martha shone like a florescent bulb. Her young, innocent face wore a dazzling, confident smile. She moved like a drifting feather and her eyes spoke of a new-born wisdom.

"How did I lose such golden memories?" Martha said in a silky smooth voice. Her usual air of anxiety had gone, along with her nervous squeak.

I don't rightly know," Brian said as his twitching eyes finally settled, "but I don't plan on letting it happen again." Gerald pointed a bony finger in Brian's direction.

"How do we do that?" He asked as he tapped the air.

"We just have to keep reminding ourselves somehow," Brian replied.

"That's not what worries me the most," Martha said as she floated around to face the other two ghosts. Barbara was beginning to feel unnoticed.

"No?" Gerald said as he lowered his finger.

"What worries me is that there might be others who are suffering ignorance as we did, both alive and dead. People who have forgotten the joy they experienced during the Christmases of their past."

"Not only that," Brian added, "there's bound to be a lot of poor souls out there who are failing to truly appreciate the present festivities."

"Are we forgetting the Christmases yet to come?" Gerald pointed out.

"We need to get out there and remind these people of the true meaning of Christmas," Martha suggested.

"I couldn't agree more," Brian said.

"Neither could I," Gerald nodded in agreement.

"That wasn't a question Gerald!" Brian observed. "You just spoke and it wasn't in the form of a question."

"Wasn't it?" Gerald asked.

"Well that didn't last long then, did it," Martha said. Barbara was getting a little tired of being ignored.

"I'm still here you know!"

"Sorry Madam Smith," Martha said as she pirouetted in mid-air to face her.

"Yes of course, sorry, Madam Smith." Brian's smile drew back across his face. It was as infectious as ever, Barbara had to fight against her own facial muscles as they attempted to return the expression.

"I take it that my plan worked."

"It did?" Gerald offered and Barbara heard it as a statement more than a question.

"Thank you Madam Smith," Brian said as he clasped his hands in front of him in a big fist which he gently shook. "You have really opened my eyes to all the joy that this festive time of year can bring to the world. I can't thank you enough in fact, you have given my death more meaning. No longer will I mope around feeling regretful at what little my life really amounted to. I will now devote my ghostly existence to bringing enlightenment and joy to any who may fail in achieving this for themselves."

"Will I follow in your footsteps and tell those who prioritise all other things above spreading goodwill through the many years to come?"

"I'm sure that you will, Gerald," Barbara replied, even though she knew there was no question of it.

"I too will join in your crusade to rid the world of bad memories by washing them away with the good," Martha said as her glow reached an intensity that Barbara had never before seen. What kind of monster have I just created, Barbara thought as a new voice entered the room.

"What's going on here then?" All eyes turned to look at the new arrival who had just stepped through the wall. He wore a pinstriped three-piece suit and stood tall and proud, while swinging a pocket watch on a long silver chain in tight circles with his right hand.

"Hello Jacob," Brian said. "Madam Smith has just reminded us of the meaning of Christmas and now we're going to spread the festive spirit with the world."

"Is that so?" Jacob said, still swinging his watch. "How do you plan on doing that then?"

"I think we are going to find miserable, lonely people and teach them to how to celebrate the festive season properly."

"That's right Brian," Martha agreed.

"Really, do you know who you are going to start with?"

"No we don't, do we?" Gerald said.

"No we don't," Brain added, "not yet."

"Then in that case, I know just the person," Jacob announced.

"Who?" Martha asked.

"My old business partner," Jacob replied, "that's who."

"Lead the way, my good man," Brian said as he headed towards Jacob and the kitchen wall.

"Wait for me," Gerald said, "are we all going in together or one at a time?"

"One at a time would be best, I think," Brian replied as he and Jacob stepped through the wall.

"I'll go first," Martha cried out as she swooped past Gerald.

"Do you want me to be last?" Gerald asked as he lumbered through the wall and disappeared from sight. Barbara sighed and switched the kettle back on. She just couldn't seem to shift the feeling of déjà vu.

.

THE END
2013 Peter John

Christmas Hope
By
Jim Murdoch

John Smith hated his name. It was such an ordinary name. Millions of John Smiths were in the phone books of all the cities he had ever been to. Why couldn't he have a more interesting name, like Bartholomew Goldstein or Winston Williams. Anything would be better than John Smith. At least with a peculiar name he could get some kind of response, even if it were only a raised eyebrow. John Smith was just ordinary, in fact it was less than ordinary. It made him feel invisible. Unknown. Unwanted. Unattractive. Uninteresting.

Out of work and feeling rejected, John was wandering in the opposite side of town. He had just endured yet another sad interview from some uneducated, know nothing stand in. What on earth are these people looking for. Nothing specific to the job was asked, just pointless chatter. Maybe it was some sort of psychological test. Well if it was, he probably failed immensely. He just wasn't in the mood for psycho tests. He wanted a job and he needed it yesterday. Being out of work just wasn't fun. John had been looking for work for six months now and every time it was the same old story: Sorry, but you are over qualified for this position. Why can't they simply be honest and say: sorry, we don't want to pay someone your age the expected salary, we'd prefer to pay a dirt cheap salary to some young college graduate who has no experience and will probably cost our company thousands in dumb mistakes.

Where to now? John Smith hated his name even more after a rejection like that. He wanted a new name. It must be his name which caused so many rejections. They just don't want such an ordinary person. The plain name was enough to put any firm off from hiring him. Hands in his pockets, he kicks a pebble along the pavement. He slumbered up to it and kicked again. The pebble bounced off a rain spout and danced into a narrow alleyway. Not wanting to pursue a pebble, John glanced down the alleyway. A few meters away lay an old battered cardboard box. As John Smith stepped forward to continue on and turned his head away from the alley something caught his eye. Did something move in that box. Maybe it's a cat or an abandoned puppy. Hmm, A little companion would be uplifting right now. Besides, it would soon Christmas and a little puppy would be just perfect to give him some Christmas Cheer.

Stopping, John turned on his heel and returned to the alleyway. He walked the few paces down to the box which was turned on its side. Something moved again. John looked inside but all he could see were some rags. Maybe rats, he thought. He prodded the rags gently with his foot. More movement and a slight groan. A tiny hand appeared and pulled down some of the rags. A tattered and dirty little girl looked up into John's eyes.

My word, thought John, a little girl. What is she doing here? The tired eyes looked up at John and the little girl offered up a weak smile.

"Hello," she said with barely an utterance.

John knelt to get a closer look at the girl.

"Hello," he answered, returning the smile. Suddenly his own trauma was forgotten. That will have to wait now. "What are you doing here?" The girl looked too weak even to speak. He placed his hand on her forehead. "Wow, you have a high fever. Where do you live? Where is your mummy?" The little girl could only look and smile and said nothing. Her eyes rolled upward and almost closed. John stood, pacing, wondering what to do. Call an ambulance. Knock on a nearby door. He remembered passing a hospital a few streets back. Stooping low John gathered the tiny bundle into his arms. "I'll get you some care. We're going to make you well again." The girl gives another weak smile.

She looked about seven years old, yet felt so light and tiny. John's heart began to thump at the thought of the girl dying. He hurried the few blocks back to the hospital. Not knowing how else to do it, he signed in the little girl with him as her guardian. He didn't know the girls name. Feeling the urgency John persuaded the staff to look at the girl first and check her name later. They took her into an emergency room. A lady doctor looked at the child and then at John. Her face carried a huge sign of concern. This didn't look good.

John was pacing again, this time in the waiting area down the hall from the emergency theater, when a nurse rushed out.

"Mr. Smith, please come." John, startled out of his thoughts of concern about the child, looked up and hurried towards the nurse. Her eyes said it all. With a shake of her head she opened the door to allow him to enter.

John hurried to the girl's side and took her cold little hand. The girl opened her eyes, still managed a smile and opened her mouth to speak. He moved closer to hear; very faint sounds emerged.

"I love you," he heard the girl say. With that she breathed her last and slipped away as quietly as she had appeared. Gone, before John could even grasp the reality of the little girl's existence. He felt a strange emotion rising from within. Gasping he held his hand over his mouth and began to sob uncontrollably. With both hands over his face, John cried out between gasps, "I don't even know who she was." The nurse was doing her best to comfort this strange man who brought the dying unknown child into the hospital.

"You did the right thing," she said not able to hold back her tears.

"There's a note in her hand," announced the doctor as she cared for the tiny corpse. John, wiping his face looked to see what the doctor had found. Crumpled in the little girl's hand was a dirty piece of paper. It was a photo of a smaller girl. On the back was written in a child's hand, "Dear John Smith, thank you for taking care of me. I love you forever. Please look after my little sister, Jen." The note was signed, "Gaby."

Puzzled, John looked at the doctor and the nurse.

"How did she know my name? I don't know any Gaby." John looked at the note, the photo, and the dead little girl. When did she write this? This isn't possible. Of course, it must be some other John Smith. After all there are millions of them. John offered to take the photo and try to find the girl's parents. He walked back to the area where he had found her lying, dying in the cardboard box. He started by asking some other children if they knew the little girl in the photo. He then asked some passersby. He walked into a couple of small stores and asked the shopkeepers. No one knew the girl in the photo or had heard of a little girl living in a box.

John walked up and down the entire area, street after street, sometimes knocking on doors, but no one recognized the photo. Exhausted he returned to the alleyway where he found the dying girl. The box was still there. John stepped up to the box in the darkness. Not really knowing why he stooped down to look into the box. He used his mobile phone to shine a little light. It was just a cardboard box, nothing special, no cushions, no blankets, no food scraps. Just a dirty cardboard box. For a strange reason he felt compelled to know what it was like for the girl to sleep here. Crouching lower he pushed himself into the box as much as he could fit. Chest, shoulders and head fitted in and he rested against the side touching the wall.

It was dark, a strange smell came from the damp cardboard and the garbage in the alleyway. A black cat strolled by. It paused in mid step to look at the strange human half stuck into a box and then moved on, showing total disinterest. Distant traffic could be heard, a shout streets away. Silence. Darkness. Stillness. Loneliness. That was it. That is what the girl felt the most and perhaps that is why John felt so much in harmony with the little girl. It was loneliness. She had been lonely. He was lonely. He was her only friend and he didn't even know her name, yet she somehow knew his. It was almost as if she knew he was coming.

But there were millions of John Smiths.

***

With a jump John woke. He was still in the box, but the darkness had given way to the light of a new day. A new day, new hopes. At least that is what he tried to tell himself every morning for the past few months. It kept him going and, even though he could no longer pay his rent, he loathed to go to the social. Maybe that's what he needed to do, or live in a box like his little girl. His little girl, he thought. He stood up, stretched and dusted down his suit with his hands. Not very interview ready now I'm afraid, John thought to himself as he looked at his wrinkled trousers. His stomach rumbled. There's got to be somewhere to get breakfast; at least he still had some money for food.

Leaving the alley, John turned towards the hospital.

There was a cafe of sorts on the way which he had seen the night before. He found it, entered, ordered coffee and scones and sat down at a table. His phone rang. It was the hospital, they wanted to know what they should do with the body. John tried to explain that he was still looking for the girl's family. Maybe they should inform the police to help. When the call ended, the proprietor came over to John.

"Excuse me, I couldn't help overhearing. You looking for a girl's family?" John looked at the enquirer.

"Yes. It's the family of a little girl who died last night. I found her lying in a box in the alleyway."

"That's sad. Is that a photo of the girl's family?" John had been flipping the photo between his fingers.

"Yes. This was found in the little girl's hand. This must be her sister."

"Hmm. Looks kind of familiar." Reaching out his hand he said, "I'm Bob. I'm the owner here." John took his hand and exchanged names. "I'll ask the customers if they know who she is."

"Oh, that would be great," thanked John. Just then a hustle of people started streaming into the cafe.

"Well, got to go. My busy time of day," Bob said as he attended to his customers. John watched as he finished his breakfast. Bob was alone and almost run off his feet. He was a little overweight and he struggled to keep up with the influx of orders.

Picking up his dishes, John brought them to the counter.

"Hey, Bob, you could use some help. Look I'm free, why don't I help a bit. Maybe we'll get a lead on the photo."

"Hey, that's kind of you, John. Of course." John took off his jacket and tie and hung them at the back of the shop.

For the few hours the little cafe was busy serving breakfasts and coffees and teas. A new delivery of fresh bread came in and John was managing taking orders, getting them ready, pouring the drinks and serving while Bob was busy with the delivery.

"I usually have help but she hasn't shown up for a while and I just haven't got a replacement." Bob apologized for the work John had to do. "I really appreciate you stepping in like that. You know, I can pay you for this. I really appreciate it." John was pouring anther coffee for a customer.

"You're welcome Bob. You know I'm finding this kinda fun. I'm out of work you know. So I don't mind stepping in until your girl gets back." Bob looked at John with a short consideration in his eyes.

"She won't be back. The job's yours for as long as you want it." John could hardly believe his ears. Here he was in his wrinkled suit and no tie and he had just been offered a job. A new day, new hopes.

"Thank you, Bob. I'll gladly take it on."

The cafe was slowly calming down after the lunch rush. The door opened and the bell above the door rang its single chime. Busy cleaning tables John didn't take any notice. He was vaguely aware of a woman and a child walking over to the counter where Bob was standing.

"Do you have any stale bread? My little girl is hungry," said the women in a very shy, perhaps embarrassed voice. John looked up to see what kind of woman would be asking for stale bread.

The woman was a sorry sight. She was haggard and thin, her hair in a mess and her clothes had more wrinkles than his. But it was the little girl at her side which caught his attention. She was only a toddler, about three years old. She was looking straight at John with a wide smile. John fumbled in his pocket and removed the photo. Yes, there was no mistaking it. This was the girl in the photo. Just then the little girl spoke out loud pointing to John.

"Are you John Smith?" John stood frozen in his tracks. Bob stood watching the trio. The woman had turned to look at John then shushed the little girl in her hand.

"Are you Jen?" John managed to ask.

"And you're John Smith," the girl said as she nodded her head

"Shh, Jen," the mother said. "Don't bother the man." Then, as if she had just suddenly realised that John had spoken her daughter's name, she looked at him with hopeful suspicion. "How do you know my daughter's name?" Bob and John's eyes met. Bob indicated that John should say nothing. He then made an eating movement with his hand before pointing to the two new guests. John understood. Bob wanted to serve them some food first, before breaking the bad news.

"Why don't you take a seat," offered John. "We'll give you something to eat. Some warm pizza to warm the little girl's tummy." The toddler was still looking at John and smiled.

"Thank you, John Smith." John said nothing and proceeded to help Bob get them some pizza. The two men kept away from the two females as they devoured the slices of pizza served to them.

Finally the mother looked up and thanked them. She was getting up to leave when John approached.

"Please wait a moment," he said as he took a seat at their table. He pulled out the photo and showed it to the woman. The woman stared then grabbed the photo. Tears welled in her eyes.

"Where did you get this?" she asked, almost demanding. Then she turned it over looking at the scribbled note then looked at John. "How did you get this? Where is my baby?" The tears were now streaming down her cheeks.

John took out his driving license and showed it to the woman. "I'm John Smith," he said matter of factly. The woman looked at the name of the license, then at the photo's note, then at John.

"I... I don't understand," she stuttered.

"Neither do I," agreed John. "I found a little girl in the alleyway last night. She was grasping this photo. Unfortunately," John could already see that his choice of word already said it all without saying. "After carrying her to the hospital, she died." John waited for the news to sink in. The woman wide eyed and silent. "That's where she is now."

Deep gasps emerged from the woman's chest, then she groaned loudly with a painful cry. She cried in pain and huge sobs as the little toddler at her side watched and kept a close eye on John. Every time she looked at John she smiled. "You are John Smith," she said shyly.

John and Bob allowed the mother to cry it out. They could only guess at the circumstances surrounding Gaby being alone on the street. For John guessed that Gaby was the name of the dead girl. Jen's big sister. Bob cleared the plates away and John took the woman's hand. "I'm sorry," he said, barely holding back his own tears. "I did what I could." The woman looked up at him, her face torn with pain and smudged with dirt and tears.

"Thank you," she said. "It's all my fault. You see when my husband left us three years ago, just after Jen was born," her loving caress on the child's head didn't go unnoticed by John or Bob, "I couldn't find permanent work then I... I started drinking." More sobs and she covered her face, her right hand still held by John. Sniffing she continued, "After two years of drinking and screaming Gaby eventually left to look for you. I haven't seen her in six weeks." John was puzzled but the woman motioned with her hand for him to wait. She went to explain.

"You see, Gaby began talking about a man who would come to save us and help us, bring us food and give us a nice home. It was fun to think about and, when I asked what was this man's name, she grabbed a phone book and opened it. There were pages and pages of Smith, John. So that was the name she picked. From then on it was John Smith this and John Smith that, and it would be John Smith who would come and save us." She paused to look at John more intently. Her mouth curled up into a wide smile, "and your name is John Smith! That's... that's..."

"Amazing! I know. I find it hard to grasp myself." John was stumped at this revelation of little Gaby's invention of her savior, John Smith. Yet Gaby appeared to know when he arrived. Or perhaps it was her faith which assumed that he was the one. Too late for Gaby, thought John, but what about her Mum and tiny Jen? They've just been fed, just as Gaby predicted in her fantasy; or was it fantasy. Looking up to Bob standing nearby John said.

"Somewhere I remember reading something about... what you hold in your mind with intense desire will eventually come about." Bob walked over to a picture on the wall and turned it around to show the reverse side. There in bright letters were painted the words: Believe and you will Receive.

"I look at those words when I feel down," admitted Bob. "It reminds me to have faith; to believe in something, to believe in what I'm doing. And what I'm doing is feeding hungry people." Bob had spoken with such passion that all three, even little Jen, were looking at him.

John was scratching his head. "Then even if it was a fantasy of Gaby's, she believed it enough and…, well here I am, here we are." John thought of the start of the previous day, how he had hated his name, yet this story with this mother and her two daughters, one now dead, were centered around that name, his name. His eyes met the mother's.

"What is your name?" he asked.

"Sue." John loves the sound of the name. He feels drawn into Sue's eyes, into her life, into her sorrow. A shake on his arm brings him back to the present.

"You are John Smith and you help us. Thank you for the pizza." Little Jen spoke loud and excited and was smiling up at John with her big eyes.

"You're welcome," he says stroking her hair.

"Where do you live?" John wanted to know. Sue looked to the ground then met John's eyes again.

"We don't have a home. I couldn't pay for one. We live in hostels and churches and such." Her cheeks flushed pink in embarrassment and she looked away. John be-wondered the woman whose life was torn apart by circumstances but it was circumstance which now offered her hope. Maybe it more than just circumstance? Gaby's story was being fulfilled before their very eyes.

John stood and looked to Bob, not knowing what to do. His own apartment was about to be reclaimed because he hadn't paid his rent in months. Bob understood. The big man smiled, placed his fists on either hip and looked at his three new friends.

"Above the shop is a two bedroom apartment waiting for new tenants. John has a job, working here, why don't you three move in up there and get that young lass some warm clothes. There's a bed there will do Jen, the rest we can find, no problem."

The offer seems too good to be true. A job, an apartment, and a family, all in one day. John couldn't hold back his pleasure, then the tears. He picked up Jen and held her in his arms. It all felt so natural, so... belonging. Jen looked at him and pointed with her tiny finger. Shrugging her shoulders, she whispered.

"You are John Smith." Sue stroked Jen's back, coming nearer. Smiling she said.

"That's right, Jen. Your sister Gaby's dream has come true and Gaby has gone to heaven." Jen wrapped her arms around John's neck.

"I love John Smith. Gaby's John Smith."

John felt the warmth of the embrace in his entire being. Such a feeling he had never known before. Sue looked relieved, Bob was ablaze at his bright idea and Jen was content in his arms. And he? John thought for a moment. Then looked to Sue, then to Bob and said.

"I love my name."

THE END
2013 Jim Murdoch

The Case of the Shiny Red Gift Box
By
Chris Raven

Charles had always loved Christmas, and despite the fact that he would only be spending it with Benedict, there were no excuses for not doing it properly, with all the trimmings. The turkey was happily defrosting in the fridge, next to a jar of homemade cranberry sauce and the veggies were all set out and ready for peeling and chopping in the morning. Charles was just starting to prepare the 'pigs-in-blankets' when the doorbell chimed.

Charles wiped his hands on a tea towel and stepped into the hallway. He quickly checked his appearance in the large ornate wall mirror and smoothed down his immaculately groomed moustache. He opened the front door and found Mike Astley standing there in his customary brown overalls. A large key chain hung from his belt and, as per usual, his wrinkled red-cheeked face looked uncomfortable as he scratched his bulbous and heavily veined nose.

"My dear Michael," Charles said warmly, offering his hand. "What can I do for you this fine Christmas Eve morning?" Charles liked the caretaker but he could never resist messing around with him.

"Morning Mr Clementine," Mike replied. His eyes darting around nervously as he gave the proffered hand a very fleeting shake. "I'm sorry to disturb you at Christmas."

"Michael, you know it's always a pleasure, but how many times must I tell you: it's Charles. Now what is that I see under your arm? A gift?"

"Oh!" Mike said. He seemed almost startled to find the small parcel still in his possession. "Yes, this is the reason I called round actually. It was found in the building, but it has no name on it; I would hate to think of some kiddie missing out on a Christmas present. So I thought, what with you knowing lots of people through the Neighbourhood Watch, you might have an idea who it belonged to."

"Oh I see," Charles said excitedly, beckoning Mike inside. "A mystery, oh good. Do come in, come in."

Charles showed Mike past the kitchen and into the sitting room, where he abruptly spun around, with a hand outstretched, to receive the parcel.

"Now then," he said, taking the gift box from Mike. "Let us see what we have here."

The Parcel was heavy, about six inches long, four inches wide and about an inch and a half deep. It was obviously a box of some sort, cardboard probably, and it was all neatly wrapped in shiny red gift paper.

"A woman wrapped this parcel I suspect," Charles announced confidently, "no man would have taken this much care and the paper is of reasonably good quality". He gave the box a gentle shake and something heavy thudded from side to side within.

"Curious," Charles declared, placing the parcel on the dining table. "Leave it with me and I'll see what I can do."

*****

Later that morning Benedict finally got out of bed and sauntered into the sitting room wearing his dressing gown. "Morning Charlie," he called out as he made his way towards the kitchen for his first mug of coffee of the day. He stopped suddenly en route as he spotted the parcel sitting on the dining table, and he stared at it for a few seconds in both shock and surprise.

"Oh, you've seen the parcel," Charles said, coming out

of the kitchen and down the hall. "Mike came round earlier with it; no one knows who owns it."

"Oh," Benedict replied, confused and still a little shocked. "I see and why do we have it?"

"We're going to discover to whom it belongs, and then we are going to return it ready for Christmas Day," he said gleefully. "It's a mystery and I'm going to be Santa Sherlock Holmes, you can be my little elfy helper.

"Charming," Benedict exclaimed, "as long as I don't have to wear green tights. Anyway, where are you going to start?"

"I don't know," Charles replied thoughtfully, "do you think we should open it?"

"No!" Benedict cried, almost little too abruptly.

"Alright, don't have a hissy, but you're right; we shouldn't ruin this nicely wrapped parcel unless we have to."

"I think we should just return it to Mike and forget all about it," Benedict said sourly.

"Oh Ben, where's your sense of adventure?" Charles chided, as he crossed the room towards the telephone. "I thought you liked a challenge."

"I do," Benedict replied, "but it's Christmas Eve."

"Don't be a scrooge, it'll be fun," Charles insisted. Not if you find out what's in it, Benedict thought.

"Who are you ringing?" He asked, as Charles picked up the telephone; it was an old-fashioned retro affair with a dial instead of buttons.

"I'm ringing the biggest gossip in the block Ben, the biggest gossip in the block."

*****

Mary Paddock was as large as her personality, which

was big, cheery and hard to ignore. She loved talking to people, which was why she bounded to the telephone as soon as it started to ring.

"Hello, Mary Paddock speaking," she announced as she picked up the receiver.

"Hello Mary, its Charles." Mary almost squealed with excitement.

"Hello Charles, how are you?" This must be important, she thought, neighbourhood watch business no doubt and urgent enough to disturb her on Christmas Eve. When Charles told her about the situation, she wasn't disappointed.

"Really!" she exclaimed, "how wonderful. This is like a real life mystery, we're like detectives."

"I know," Charles replied, "so what do you think?"

"Shiny red wrapping paper you said," Mary scratched her head in thought. "I've seen it for sale somewhere."

"Downstairs?" Charles enquired. "Maybe in one of the retail units down on the ground floor?" Mary suddenly clicked her fingers.

"The mini-mart," she announced, "I've seen it in the mini-mart!"

*****

Twenty minutes later an excited Charles and Mary were stamping their feet in the swirling snow and rubbing their gloved hands together while they waited outside the mini-mart for Benedict to join them. Benedict eventually arrived, wrapped from head to foot in a large overcoat. His collar was upturned over a thick scarf that was wrapped round his neck, jaw and nose; he looked like a highwayman. His eyes were just visible between the scarf and a woollen beanie hat. Even with only a fraction of his face visible, there was no mistaking his acrid mood.

"I really don't want to be here," he said glumly. "I think this is a complete waste of time."

"Is Benedict alright?" Mary quietly asked Charles, as they walked towards the shop doorway.

"Don't mind him," Charles replied brightly, "he's not been up long and he's never been a morning person, have you sweetie". Benedict gave him two fingers.

"That is not very Christmassy Ben," Charles laughed, as he led the way into the warmth of the shop.

They found a small dust-covered supply of stationery, in a rarely visited section of an aisle, at the very back of the shop. Hidden amongst the envelopes, writing pads, ball-point pens and greeting cards was indeed a large supply of shiny wrapping paper. There was a variety of different colours but none of them were red. A quick enquiry with Mr Atalar, the Mini-mart's owner, and the would-be detectives learnt that the last of the red paper had been sold out. It had been mainly bought by two people: Vic Hollis at the shoe repair shop and Bert the Bouncer, manager of the 'Pies and Tarts' restaurant just around the block in the next street.

Benedict appeared to perk up a bit. He suggested that they split up to save time and meet later at the coffee shop to exchange notes. The three of them then left the mini-mart and headed back the way they had come. Turning a corner, they approached the black and gold fronted restaurant and Benedict ran ahead and pushed open the door.

"I'll see you two in a little while then," he said cheerfully, and then disappeared inside, leaving Charles and Mary to continue round the block toward Hollis'.

*****

When Charles and Mary entered his shop, Vic Hollis was

stooped over his work station repairing a large brown work boot. He looked up and regarded them both through thick glasses that magnified his eyes to the point of making him look perpetually startled. Long grey hair framed the sides of his face but the top of his head was completely bald and as shiny as the parcel that Charles was holding in his hand. Vic gradually rose to his feet and Charles could hear the old man's knees creaking. Vic slowly walked down the length of the counter to where his new 'customers' were waiting for him; he did not seem pleased to see them.

"What can I do for you?" He said gruffly and Charles showed him the parcel.

"We were wondering if this was yours or if you know anything about it?" He asked.

"Nope," was the curt reply. Vic made no attempt to take the parcel from Charles when he offered it for inspection.

Charles hesitated for a second and then enquired further.

"You bought some red wrapping paper from the mini-mart recently, just like the paper on this parcel."

"I did," Vic replied. The conversation faltered again.

"May we ask what you wanted it for?" Mary cut in and Vic slowly turned his owl-like eyes towards her.

"Yes," he said. Charles and Mary waited for Vic to continue; a prolonged silence filled the shop.

"And?" Charles eventually asked.

"You can ask," Vic explained, "though it doesn't mean I'm going to answer."

Charles and Mary exchanged bewildered looks.

"We're sorry," Mary finally apologised, "we didn't mean to be rude; it's just that we are trying to return this parcel to its rightful owner before Christmas Day." Vic appeared to study them for a moment or two and then his expression softened a little.

"Parcel's not mine, don't know anything about it. Had presents of my own to send to family in Australia. Is that what you wanted to know?"

"Yes it is," Mary said gratefully, "and thank you very much for your time."

*****

Benedict eventually joined Charles and Mary in Clio's Coffee shop, where they both looked up expectantly when he joined them at their table. The cute redhead, whose make-up would have caused a drag queen to pause, was working behind the counter and called out when she saw him at the table.

"Hi Benedict, the usual?"

"Yes please Jan," Benedict replied. He sat down next to Mary and looked across the table to Charles, grinning.

"You took your time," Charles said, clearly frustrated. "Did you get anywhere?"

"All sorted," Benedict announced smugly. "The parcel belongs to a waitress in the pie shop and we can return it to her on our way home." Charles and Mary looked at each other ecstatically.

"You see Ben, wasn't that fun," Charles said. "What a wonderful way to spend Christmas Eve."

"Actually, it was," Benedict conceded truthfully and thought about how lucky he had been.

That had been a close shave. The parcel sitting on the table in front of Charles had not, as Benedict had originally assumed, been for him. He knew that he was due a gift, as Bert in the 'Pie Shop' had let it slip some weeks earlier, saying that as a loyal customer he could expect a little something 'to show our appreciation'. So when Benedict saw the parcel on the dining table that morning, he thought that he would have a lot of explaining to do. He had not believed his luck when the opportunity arose to talk to Bert in private. That conversation had also prevented his own parcel from being delivered to him later that day.

Benedict sipped the coffee that Jan had just brought over, and patted the box in his coat pocket. He felt the weight of the fluffy, pink fur covered handcuffs shift inside. In his other pocket was a glittery Christmas card, which he had also received from Bert, thanking him for his continued patronage of a certain private club that existed in the back of the 'members only' pie restaurant. A club that offered certain services that Benedict would prefer that Charles remained blissfully unaware of, especially today.

Well, it wouldn't do to spoil Charles' Christmas now, would it.

THE END
2013 Chris Raven

Glimpse
By William O'Brien

Days did pass
Knowledge given
The previous year
A wished for present

Failing to find
One true path
Moonbeams shimmer
Through stained glass

Wanting to heal
Unfortunate and lost
Though not so easy
As stones are cast

Long cobbled road
A journey so long
Wanting to go
Right back home

The time now placed
And patience learned
Reward of magic
Entwines the lands

Hot golden sprays
From a dragon's breath
Mounting the seat
Shows the quest
***

© 2013 William O'Brien

A Coast to Coast Paranormal Investigations Christmas Story
The Perfect Gift
By Carolyn Bennett

It was early December and, as usual, it was sunny and a balmy 70 degrees in Vegas. My team, Coast to Coast Paranormal Investigations, was on a break from ghost hunting until the middle of January as was Aaron's team: The Spirit Chasers.

We stood in the living room of our modest Las Vegas bungalow, setting up our Christmas tree. It took me two years to convince Aaron to get a bigger tree. At first he didn't see the point of it, insisting on pulling out his old Charlie Brown-like tree from the basement.

"Babe, this is Vegas, we don't get snow, heck most of the time we are either having a barbeque or a party out in the desert. I don't see the point in spending money on an artificial tree.

"Because it reminds me of what Christmas was like in Ontario, before I came here. Please Aaron it would mean so much to me." The following week we went on a road trip and finally found a beautiful artificial 8ft douglas fir.

As we finished putting up the last of the new decorations, we were distracted by the sound of our daughter, Amelia Grace, huffing and grunting while she dragged a box down the hall from her bedroom to the living room.

Amelia Grace Greyson has been a going concern since her premature birth over five years ago. To watch her now you would never know how close we came to losing her that night or that she was born smaller than average and needed oxygen to help her breathe the first couple weeks. Once she began to grow she just took off and never looked back. She has never stopped; she's into everything, exploring everything and testing every possible limit she can.

Oh dear, what is she up to now, I wondered to myself. I could tell by the look on Aaron's face that he was thinking the same thing.

When she finally reached the living room she stopped and looked at the two of us, hands fisted into her hips.

"You could have helped," she scolded us.

"Amelia, what are you doing?"

"These are the toys I don't play with anymore. I'm giving them away."

I sat on the ottoman next to her and examined the contents of the box. It included a variety of dolls, stuffed animals and an assortment of other toys.

"Are you sure, there's a lot in here. I hope you are not expecting to have them all replaced at Christmas."

She gave me the look. The look she inherited from her father; that ability to raise only one eyebrow when she was annoyed about something.

"I still have lots of toys left, besides, you and daddy and uncle Aiden and Scott always get a little carried away at Christmas."

"Yes we do, and Uncle Scott and Aiden more so, but that's because everyone loves you so darn much," I laughed.

"I know mommy but I don't need all these toys; I want to do something special with them."

"Okay, are we going down to the fire hall to donate them?"

"We're taking these to Claire," she said, shaking her head.

"Claire?" I hesitated. "Does she go to your school?"

"No mommy, Claire!"

By now Aaron had sat next to us, he draped his arm

gently over my shoulder.

"What do you mean baby girl? Who is Claire?" he asked.

I could tell she was frustrated by us not understanding what she meant but then it suddenly came to me.

"Amelia, do you mean Claire from Kentucky?" She nodded sheepishly, in silent reply.

When Amelia was four I fulfilled a promise I made two years previously and brought her to Waverly Hills Sanatorium in Louisville, Kentucky, to meet Claire. It wasn't like we took her on an investigation with us. We may both be paranormal investigators but we are not crazy.

Claire is the spirit of a young girl that died at Waverly Hills after a short battle with tuberculosis. She came to me during my second investigation at the hospital. I had taken ill just before the investigation and, during the evening, I had collapsed from dehydration and nausea. I had not realized that I was pregnant and it was Claire who had first told me.

"Don't worry, she'll be fine. Can you bring her back to play with us?" At first I hadn't understood what she meant but then I had heard the sound of a baby crying and I assumed she was looking for a younger sister, who may have also passed away from the virus. It wasn't until we returned home that we had discovered that Aaron and I were expecting what would be our only child.

Amelia is our miracle baby. Doctors had told me years earlier that it was not likely I could ever get pregnant again. Then, just shy of 34 weeks into the pregnancy, I suffered a traumatic medical emergency. Amelia and I had almost died. It was by the hands of the skilled doctors and the grace of God that we are both alive today.

I returned to Waverly for another investigation two years

later. Claire was waiting for me on the fifth floor but she kept her back to me and would not speak to me as she sulked in the corner. Finally, when she turned, I could tell she had been crying.

"Claire, what's wrong?" Yes I realized I was speaking with a spirit child.

"You promised you would bring her. I want to see her, you promised."

I knelt in front of her; I tried to comfort her by caressing her arm but my hand simply passed through her translucent body.

"Claire I will, I promise, but she's too young yet; she's only 2 years old. I need you to be patient. I will bring her when she's older, I promise. Besides, you can't play with her yet; she's so much smaller than you and your friends."

"No you won't. It's just like everyone else who left us here and forgot us."

"Claire, you know that's not true. I come back every year to see you. When Amelia is older, I promise I will bring her."

"When?" Claire said and I could tell that she was going to pin me down to a commitment.

"When she is four years old."

"That will take forever!"

"No Claire it won't. Time is different for me and you. What is two years for us would only see like moments for you. Do you remember how long you have been here?"

"A long time" she answered as she sniffled again.

"Does it feel like it has been over 70 years?"

"No, don't be silly, I'm only 12." She laughed and shook her head at me.

"I know Claire, you will have to trust me that we will be back when Amelia is four and it won't seem that long to you."

She nodded her head, turned to join her friends who were waiting on the newly finished outdoor playroom, and disappeared.

Two years later we arranged to bring Amelia for her first visit to Claire and Waverly Hills.

I contacted Tracy, the owner, to let her know I was coming for a daytime visit and bringing Amelia. At first she thought I was crazy but she had also seen the spirit of Claire and had been there the night that she made her presence known to me.

At first Amelia was afraid of the large and very gothic looking building. Tucked away on the side of a hill, Waverly hardly looked inviting but, once we got out of our truck, she immediately pointed to the fifth floor.

"Mommy who is that?"

I glanced up and there was Claire, grinning like a silly school girl.

"That's Claire. Do you remember what I told you about Claire?"

Amelia nodded.

"Claire is very lonely here and wants to meet you. You don't need to be afraid; she won't hurt you but she will look different."

"I know mommy," and off we went.

Since that visit I've had the feeling that Claire had somehow attached herself to Amelia before we left. I don't believe she followed us home but I suspect that Claire has been speaking with Amelia, within her mind. At school the teacher had noticed prolonged periods where Amelia seems to be focused on something else. Even at home, she would spend time in her room playing with imaginary friends.

However, they might not be imaginary friends. Children

are the most open to spirit communication. Their young minds have not yet been influenced by those who either don't believe or are afraid of the unknown.

"Well?" She poked me, as if irritated that I was lost in thought.

"I don't know Amelia. It's quite a drive to bring toys. Are you sure we can't just donate them here in Vegas?"

"No mommy." She was practically in tears. "Claire is very sad. All the kids there are. No one remembers them at Christmas. She said people only go to see if they are real but no one stays or plays with them. I don't like Claire being sad, she's my friend."

I pulled Amelia close and hugged her. I was not sure if it was the result of her near death at birth, or if she was sensitive to spirits like me, but Amelia was definitely not like other children. Things that most people would not give a second thought to upset her intensely.

"Please mommy, this is what I want to do for Christmas. I don't want any gifts from you and daddy, please" she pleaded.

Aaron knelt down and wrapped his arms around both of us.

"What do you want to do babe?"

"It's over a full day's drive there and then back again. I suppose we could find someplace to stay along the way there and back. We can make a little mini family vacation out of it."

"Maybe on the way back we can swing south and visit dad in Phoenix for a couple days. The doctor said he's almost over his bout of pneumonia but I'd like to see for myself" suggested Aaron.

"But that would mean taking Amelia out of school for a full week!"

"Babe, she's in kindergarten, it's not like she won't get accepted into university because of it."

Amelia's eyes, although a dark slate blue like her father, shone brightly with delight, sensing victory was near. Then again I almost never won when they ganged up on me.

"Please mommy."

I looked over at Aaron, he nodded.

"I have to call Tracy first and make sure it's ok. If she agrees, we'll do it."

Amelia threw her arms around my neck and hugged me tight. "Thank you, mommy."

"Hey what about me?"

"Oh daddy thank you," she said, as she released her death grip on my neck and latched on to her father.

"Ok. Are you sure you want to give all these toys to the children at Waverly?"

She nodded and held out her hand.

"And this," she said, as she gave him $10. She had received it in a birthday card from Aiden's mother. Ellen Lawson had always treated Amelia like her own grandchild and, since she assumed her son and his partner, Scott, would never have children of their own, she doted on Amelia like a true grandmother.

"What's this for Amelia?"

"It's my money from nana Ellen, daddy. I want to go shopping and buy more toys. There are a lot of kids there," she said, giving us a look like we were silly to not understand.

Our little Amelia, at times a true five year old but then there were times she seemed much older.

A few days later we ventured into the biggest toy store in town with Amelia and her $10. When we finished, Aaron carried her to the car as I pushed our cart full of balls, cars, bears and dolls through the check out. I handed the clerk Amelia's $10 bill, she had made me promise, and my credit card.

We set out the following weekend for our drive to Waverly Hills. Thankfully the weather held up as we made our way to Kentucky. Tracy, who still thought I was out of my mind, was thrilled to see us. She ran out, gave me a big hug and then bent down to shake Amelia's hand.

"Hi Amelia. Do you remember me? I was here when you came last year."

"Yes, you're the lady Claire likes. She says you take care of her and the other kids. She's happy you are here."

Tracy looked up at me and I could see tears swelling in her eyes. Her plan had always been to restore Waverly Hills into a luxury hotel/spa/resort, with the exception of the fifth floor. It would be totally renovated for the children of Waverly. It would be closed off to the hotel guests but, if the children agreed, investigators would still be allowed in. Since it was the money they paid to come to Waverly that kept the place open, she didn't want to shut them out.

There had been several times she thought she was going to have to sell the building, unable to keep up with maintenance and renovation cost. Even with opening the building up to paranormal investigations she struggled to make ends meet. Then, one day, she was approached by a production company. They wanted to film a paranormal movie in her building. It was a difficult decision. The last thing she wanted was a bunch of people disrespecting the spirits of her building.

Before deciding she went up to the fifth floor and talked with Claire and the other children. They understood that the money this would bring in would allow her to continue to renovate the building and she would not have to sell it.

Tracy met with the production company and had one non-negotiable condition: no one was allowed to go up to the fifth floor. If she found anyone disrespecting the children she'd shut them down immediately and keep their deposit.

With the contract signed, the production company spent three months on site filming what was to become one of the biggest paranormal movies of all times. They were already in negotiations with Tracy to film a sequel. Tracy's project to restore Waverly would be safe for several more years.

When we arrived Tracy, Amelia and I went to the first floor gift shop where she had a selection of cookies and juice for Amelia. We ate our cookies while Aaron unloaded the bags of toys from the back of our SUV.

"Wow," she whistled, "you weren't kidding. Are all these toys yours Amelia?"

"Yes but I also gave mommy and daddy $10 to buy more. You have a lot of children here."

Tracy laughed. "Yes we do Amelia, and I have a surprise for you and your mommy. Come on let's help your dad get these up to the fifth floor and I'll show you."

"I was thinking what you said the last time you were here Leigh, about the spirits being in the here and now and not living in the past. I realized we don't have anything for them here. Nothing. So we've spent the last year renovating part of the children's wing. I hope you like it."

The first room we entered had been redecorated as a play room. There were small chairs, rocking chairs, toys and books. There were colorful murals painted on the new walls. Tracy had set up a stand to hold the Christmas tree we brought with us.

"Tracy this is beautiful, I am sure the children will love it."

"Wait there's more." She smiled as she led us down the

south hall where two patient rooms had been converted to one larger bedroom. Inside the room was six brand new children's beds, one small dresser and a floor mirror. "I know it seems a bit much but you really had me thinking when you were here last year. I really want the children of Waverly to be happy here, this is their home."

We went back to the play room and Tracy and I watched as Amelia and Aaron carefully unpacked the toys and placed them under the tree. Amelia found her Katie doll. It had been her favorite, given to her as a birthday gift from her Uncle Aiden. He's not really her uncle, he is my best friend, but he treats her like his own. Worse, he treats her like his niece and spoils her constantly. She hugged it tight then looked at me.

"This one is for Claire, which bed is hers?"

"Here I'll show you" Tracy said as she led Amelia down to the children's bedroom. On the wall over one bed, was small plaque with the name 'Claire' on it. Carefully Amelia gave Katie doll a kiss and sat her on Claire's pillow. She looked up at me, she seemed quite proud of herself.

We finished walking the fifth floor, as Tracy proudly showed us the other renovations that were taking place, before we returned to the play room. Aaron, Tracy and I sat in the rocking chairs while Amelia played with the toys. She was talking and I am sure it was the children of Waverly that she was speaking to.

"Are you sure," I heard her whisper. "Okay I will ask mommy."

"Ask me what baby girl?"

"It's Claire, she wants to talk to you but she wants to be alone."

"Okay, is Claire in here or has she left?"

"She's gone over to her bed. She's waiting for you

there."

As I got up, Aaron reached for my hand.

"Do you want me to come with you babe?"

"No Aaron, it will be fine. I've spoken with Claire many times." He nodded at me and I left the toy room.

As I entered the bedroom, I could see a figure on the last bed. It was a girl, about 12 years old, wearing a white dress, stockings and black shoes. She had long blond hair which was tied up in pony tails. It was Claire, wearing the exact same clothes as she has for the last five years. Actually I am sure she has been wearing those same clothes since the day she passed but she seemed different today. Then I noticed something odd; she was holding the doll Amelia gave her.

I sat on the foot of the bed and carefully reached up and touched her knee. "Claire how is this possible? How can I be touching you now?"

She smiled at me and then yawned.

"I've been working really hard on this. I knew you would come with Amelia and I really wanted to play with the toys she brought but it takes so much energy and I am very tired. I am going to have a nap with Katie doll. She's cute isn't she? Amelia is very lucky; she has a very nice mommy and daddy. You take good care of her and buy her things. Not like us; no one comes and brings us things except for Tracy and you and Amelia." I could see sadness in her dark eyes.

"Don't be upset with your parents. You must realize that they have probably passed themselves and, when you got sick, people did not believe in spirits or that we could talk to them like you and I do. I am sure if your mommy knew she could do that she would have."

Claire nodded but I could tell she was not entirely convinced. I reached my arms out and she crawled down the bed and hugged me. It was an amazing feeling. It felt like energy running through my body from head to toe. She giggled, knowing it tickled me. I kissed her forehead and sat her back on the bed.

"Now Claire, sometimes children have more than one mommy or daddy. It's very sad but your mommy and daddy have probably crossed over by now. I think as long as you stay here you should think of Tracy as your new mom. She takes care of you and you are both learning how to communicate with each other, it helps her better understand what you need. She loves you like you were her own child; she loves all the children here."

Claire sat there, staring at me with wide eyes, almost like she didn't quite understand what I was saying. Then a look of amazement filled her tiny face and her sadness seemed to disappear.

"If Tracy is my new mom, does that make you my aunt? I used to have an aunty as well, three of them actually. They were really nice to me until I came here, then I never saw them again."

"Oh Claire I would like that very much."

"Aunty Leigh?" She seemed to be testing how it sounded. Looking up at me she gave me a giant grin. "Merry Christmas, Aunty Leigh. Thank you for the presents. This is my favorite," she said as she laid down, cradling Katie doll in her arms.

"Merry Christmas Claire." I got up and gave her a kiss on the head, then she disappeared.

"Merry Christmas Claire," I whispered again. I suddenly realized that this was the gift Claire truly wanted, a family of her own.

THE END
2013 Carolyn Bennett

On Christmas Day
By
Alan Hardy

Will had just come out of hospital. It had been something of a shock, feeling really, really old, maybe for the first time. He'd found it difficult to get dressed and undressed; his fingers had fumbled over slotting buttons into their elusive holes. The nurses had had to help him. Of course, when the chest infection had started to fade, things had got better. When he was discharged, and arrived home, for all intents and purposes he was back to normal. But he knew the episode was a sign of what was to come, the inexorable passing of the years.

He was thrilled to be back with Maria. Various relatives and friends had mucked in to look after her while he was away, but he had always worried about her. Perhaps that was why the infection had taken so long to clear. When he had walked into the living-room and seen her lying in her special reclining-armchair, infirm and frail, but still to him as beautiful as ever, the tears had welled up in his eyes. For a moment he had been rendered speechless, the words dying in his throat.

Once everybody had left, he sat by her in his chair, and sighed happily. Here they were again, side by side, the television flickering away in an unobserved corner, and her old family photos in their customary places on the mantelpiece; all was well with the world. Despite her ever-increasing dementia, her hand stirred shakily, searching for his hand. He took hold of it tenderly, happy to feel the softness of her flesh upon him. When in the hospital, he had feared that such a moment would never come again.

Now he was back with her, just in time for Christmas. Christmas Day was only Christmas Day when spent together with Maria. He turned to look into her blue eyes.

"Everything OK, old girl?"

She stared back at him, her face pinched and worn, but, to him, not so different from the cheeky, expressive features of the black-haired girl who had captivated him in Rome all those years ago. They'd married a few years after the end of the war and, once he'd got his demob papers, he brought her to England.

All those years ago! How the time had passed! Years of joy and, it must be said, moments of sadness and anguish, as occur in all lives, which they had survived together. They'd never had children—that had been the biggest chagrin of all—but the intensity of their love had made up for that. Even though for the last few years Maria had been slipping more and more into a voiceless blackness, Will still felt he had so much to live for. He was Maria's voice, he was her sight, he was her hearing, he was the person who sat by her side and held her hand, and he would be there for her for as long as she needed him.

There were still a few weeks left to prepare for Christmas Day. He'd managed quite a lot before he fell ill, but there was more to be done. He had to fulfil the promise he had made to Maria. She had murmured her request to him months ago. Straining to hear her words as he bent his aching back low over her, he had nodded. He had granted her wish.

"Will…please…I want to see my sisters one more time, this Christmas…"

"Of course, my dear…"

She still now spoke the occasional word, and clutches of words, but they were punctuated by long stretches of silence, and, occasionally, bouts of rambling incoherence. So, he felt, it was important to keep his promise. He'd made that promise when her mind still had a certain strength, and her words had real meaning. He knew she would hold him to it, and he wouldn't let her down.

Maria was the eldest of the six sisters. Two of the others also lived in England. They'd come to visit Maria at different times, met their future husbands, and stayed. It wasn't difficult to contact them. He had arranged for them to visit on Christmas Day. One was still in robust good health; he had to arrange a taxi for the other one, now a poorly widow in a residential care home, but he didn't mind. He didn't have that much money, but was happy to spend it to bring joy to his wife. Now back at home, he traced two of the others, who were still in Italy. He rang them up and explained in his faltering Italian what he wanted, or rather what Maria wanted. One of them immediately said she would fly over. The other one didn't sound so keen, complaining about the distance and her aches and pains, but, when he said he would buy the ticket and send it to her, she said she would travel any number of kilometres to see her dear Maria one more time.

So, that much was settled and arranged. The last sister, though, Clarissa, presented the biggest problem. Maybe it was insurmountable. She was Maria's favourite. Born just two years after her, they'd grown up together. Will remembered, when he had been courting Maria all those years ago, how she'd always brought Clarissa along as her chaperone. He'd got on famously with her. She was pretty, shorter than Maria, and always joking and laughing. She looked up to Will as the older brother she had never had. She learnt a lot from him, good things like how to behave properly, and which fork to use first, and also bad things like smoking. For those few years in Italy they had always been together, such that Will used to call them The Three Musketeers.

No, Maria would be very disappointed if Clarissa didn't come. He knew that. But that presented him with the biggest problem of them all, and he didn't know how he could possibly find an answer to it. You see, Clarissa had been dead for forty years. She'd died of leukaemia. He'd often wondered whether he had been to blame for that. She'd smoked like a trooper all her short life, and he'd been the one who introduced her to that. But then, those were different times, everybody smoked. But, if he could go back, he would undo what he had done. If only one could do that...undo what was done.

He thought and thought about it, but just couldn't hit upon a solution. Dead was dead. He couldn't bring someone back from the grave. It couldn't be done.

In the end, he hit upon a deception. He didn't like it, but he had to do something. He'd noticed, as Maria became more and more confused, and her memories sketchier and sketchier, that the collection of photographs around her seemed to acquire a life of their own for her. He had at first started to pick up the old black-and-white photos of her mother, father and sisters, and show them to her, holding them close to her face, as a means of aiding her memory, attempting to slow down the rate of its deterioration, and its eventual total loss. Then he'd noticed that at times Maria would confuse the photos with the real thing, and imagine the photo of her father, for example, in his First World War Italian Army uniform, youthful and upright, was in actual fact her father in person. She would talk to him. He didn't like to deceive her but he decided that on Christmas Day he would place Clarissa's smiling photo on the coffee-table in front of Maria and, hopefully, she would think that it was really Clarissa come to visit her after all these years. It was obvious, with Maria often speaking with her mother and father, or rather their photos, as if they were still alive, that she had forgotten they had died. Will felt that the Maria of old, the Maria he had run through the yellow corn-fields outside Rome with, laughing and joking, with the hot sun on their faces as if it would shine on them forever, until the end of the world, well, he felt that that Maria would have understood, and would have forgiven him for what he was going to do.

The days leading up to Christmas were not as enjoyable as other years. He normally found the meagre preparations his budget allowed him quite exciting, putting up sprigs of holly, spreading out the few Christmas cards they received on shelves and tables, putting up a few decorations, and, of course, their small, battered-looking tree. It wasn't just that Maria couldn't really share in the fun, it was more that Will dreaded the advent of Christmas Day because he felt he had failed her. She would be disappointed, not only because Clarissa wouldn't be there, but because he would be deliberately tricking her. And, even if Maria herself didn't manage to see through his ruse, he would know, and that awareness filled him with immense sadness. He felt he was letting her down for the first time in his life. It was like he was cheating on her.

On Christmas Day he got up with a heavy heart. While the carers were getting Maria ready, dressing her in her best clothes, he carefully placed Clarissa's photo on the coffee-table in front of Maria's reclining-chair. Images of the day of Clarissa's funeral, the family grief, and in particular Maria's distress, came to mind. Clarissa had been buried in the family tomb in the small mountain-village, just outside

Rome, which Will had spent so much time in, and grown to love over the years. He remembered the heat of that day despite the touch of breeze which had stirred up the dust, blowing it into their eyes, as they trudged mournfully along the track toward the cemetery.

The two sisters still living in Italy had arrived the previous night, while the two living in England would be coming shortly.

* * *

Will sat in the room beside Maria. They were alone. The two sisters living in England had been and gone, while the two sisters from Italy were already in bed. Their return flight was early the next morning. The day had gone relatively well with lots of tears and hugs. The joy and sadness of reunion. All the sisters looked compassionately and tenderly upon the prone figure of Maria, at times shaking their heads. Will had cried with them. Every now and then he would nudge the photo on the coffee-table, even once or twice picked it up on an excuse, when reminiscing or pretending to scratch away a mark he'd spotted, in order to give the illusion of movement, or even life. He spoke about Clarissa, and manoeuvred the conversation to get the sisters to mention her also. Whether Maria was ever duped even for a moment into thinking Clarissa was there, he doubted. All the time he was aware of Maria casting him intent glances, raising her head from her prone position on her chair. What those glances meant, whether they were accusing him of betrayal, or were merely expressing her puzzlement as to why Clarissa hadn't yet come, he didn't know. For a rare moment in his life, he avoided meeting her eyes, the eyes whose gaze he had once so willingly met and wilted under.

He sat there quietly, looking away from Maria. His

glance fell upon Clarissa's photo. He swallowed hard. He felt sure Maria was about to ask him why Clarissa hadn't come. He felt a great shame. His hand moved towards the photo. There was a knock on the front door. He went to answer it, glad to be able to run away. He answered the door unthinkingly.

"Hello, Clarissa," he said.

Clarissa hugged him, and kissed him on the cheek, as she always used to, standing on tip-toe to stretch up to him, though not quite as much as before. Will was only too aware that he was beginning to droop more and more.

Maria's eyes lit up as he led Clarissa into the room. She raised her hands, usually so limp, together in an excited, child-like clap.

Will left them alone most of the evening, only occasionally interrupting them to bring in cups of tea, mince pies and tangerines. Will felt a tug at his heart whenever he saw Maria's excited expression and demeanour. Her eyes were aflame as she lay there listening to Clarissa reminiscing about old times. Years seemed to have fallen away from her. And Clarissa, well, Clarissa looked exactly the same as in his youth. Every now and then Maria would cast Will an appreciative glance, and Will, his heart bursting, felt that if he had to die, then now would not be a bad time.

He did have a quick, private word with Clarissa just as she was leaving.

"Everything's OK where you are, is it, my dear?" he asked.

"It's wonderful, Will. Don't worry."

"Thank you so much for coming. You've made Maria's day."

"I wouldn't have missed it for the world."

* * *

So, that was it, then. The terrible things that happen, or have happened, don't need to, or can be remedied. Will knew that he had discovered something very important. It wasn't so much that he could make Clarissa live again, or cancel out her death and bring her back to life, he knew that he wasn't God or anything, but it was possible to do things for a while, maybe just a few hours, which had seemed impossible before. He suddenly had a glimpse in his mind of Maria and himself walking together hand in hand through the golden corn-fields of Italy on a blazing-hot day. That was it, moments and experiences which seemed now forever beyond their grasp were still attainable. What had seemed beyond reach was, for some reason, now within the orbit of Will and his beloved Maria.

It came into his head that he wanted, for one more time, to be a few hours with Maria when they were both still young and full of life, when Maria could jump and run and cover his face with her sweet kisses, when his body ached with boundless love, and Maria's touch was like the caress of an angel on his skin.

How could he make that happen? How had he made Clarissa arrive? What was it which caused her miraculous appearance? He moved over to the window, feeling dizzy, an occurrence which had started to worry him over the last few months. He looked out at the charming street-scene, the street-lamps casting eerie glimmers and shadows over the blanket of virginal snow. He felt he would faint at the beauty of the street on this day.

The answer came to him. It was simple. It was Christmas Day, and on Christmas Day he could make happen whatever he wanted to happen. This startling realization enervated his whole body. He had to sit down and catch his breath. Next Christmas he and Maria would, just for a while, be young again and walk hand in hand through that heart-rending, snow-covered street. All they had to do was wait for next Christmas. They had to survive the year. Simple, yet still a tall order.

It was something to keep him going throughout the year, counting off the days, weeks and eventually months to the next Christmas. At times he thought he wouldn't make it, especially when he had a couple more of those severe infections which kept him bed-ridden, and he experienced more and more of those dizzy spells. Maria, on the other hand, although there was only one slope to slide slowly down once dementia had set in, proved to be remarkably resilient over the year. Physically, she was fine, lying on her reclining-chair with a big smile on her face, eating well, generally silent, just the odd moment of rambling loquacity. Will felt sure seeing Clarissa again last Christmas had revivified her and set her up nicely for the coming year. That's what kept him going, the desire to arrange the next wonderful surprise for Maria. He would whisper it in her ear, and her eyes would light up, and her hand would give a special squeeze to his.

"We're going to be young again on Christmas Day, my darling," he would murmur. "We're going to walk hand in hand through the snow, and watch our breaths curling through the air. I'm going to throw snowballs at you, we'll make a snow-man, and come home freezing cold, and warm ourselves up by the log-fire, and roast chestnuts. My darling, we'll be young again for a whole day."

And that's how it turned out. Will had been particularly concerned on Christmas Eve when, drawing back the curtains every five minutes, he had seen no trace of snow. Imagine his delight when, looking out of the window the next morning, his eyes smarted from the expanse of whiteness that greeted him. The whole street had been softened and smoothed by a massive fall of snow during the night. He ran down the stairs to tell Maria, and then suddenly stopped still half-way down, his hand gripping the banister. He raced back up the stairs to the bedroom. He stared in the mirror. A stranger stared back. It was Will, and it wasn't Will. It was the Will of sixty, even seventy years ago. He hurried out of the room, and bounded down the stairs.

"Maria, where--?"

The words died in his throat as he was met by the sight of a tall, lithe, black-haired beauty advancing towards him, arms outstretched. It was his Maria, the Maria he had met and loved all those years ago in Italy when she had been so dazzled by his British Army uniform and he had been so dazzled by everything of her. They fell into each other's arms.

They wandered through the snow-clad street, kissed under the street-lights in the darkening afternoon, and, as their lips disengaged and they drew back from each other, he gazed deep into the intoxicating splendour of her luminous, blue eyes.

They sat by the fireside, roasting and eating chestnuts, sharing each chestnut, taking turns to feed the other. She sat in his lap, her legs dangling playfully and kicking at the coal-scuttle as the flickering flames were reflected in her eyes and reddened her cheeks, just as had happened all these years ago in a small village just outside Rome when her mother and sisters had finally gone off to bed and left them alone.

* * *

So, he could always wish for something on Christmas

Day, and it would come true. It was enough to keep him alive throughout the rest of the year. He spent the first few months of the new year pondering what his next wish could be. Many a day he spoke about it with Maria, putting forward many alternatives, and she listened with a broad, infectious smile on her lips. It didn't matter that the carers were coming more and more, and that they spent all their time together sitting side by side in the living-room, holding hands, and gazing with disinterest at the television with its flickering images in the corner of the room. They had so much to live for. They had Christmas, in particular Christmas Day, when whatever they wished for was possible.

One day he got a tremendous idea about what that wish could be this year. He hurried downstairs to speak about it with Maria, as fast as his aching legs permitted him. He was so excited by his idea that he didn't notice, when he entered the room, that Maria was bent a little more than usual to the right in her reclining-chair, her head hanging down somewhat, dishevelled grey hair touching the arm-rest of the adjacent armchair he always sat in. Excitedly he started speaking to Maria about his plan. Then he stopped. The words choked in his throat and died in the air. There was a mighty thump on his heart. On faltering legs he rushed over to her. His fingers grazed her sweet, tender face. He felt her forehead. She felt a little cold. He ran his fingers through her hair. Bending down his awkward old body, he showered her lifeless face with kisses. Taking his accustomed chair by her side, he took her limp hand in his. There he would sit, he decided, by the side of his Maria, until the carers came. That was where he belonged. He would stay there with her in her death, as he had in her life. Sitting there, with his Maria, the tears streaming down his face, he knew that his own life had also ended.

*　*　*

Life was a constant uphill struggle over the next year. Chest infection followed chest infection, hospital stay followed hospital stay, and bout of dizziness followed bout of dizziness. He kept quiet about the latter, however, as he feared the doctors wouldn't allow him to stay alone at home if they knew how wobbly he was on his feet. And he had to stay at home in order for his wish for Christmas Day to come true. He had wished for Maria to come alive again on that day. He just had one day in the year to live for, one day to wait for. And it could only happen here in his own home. He knew that.

The days before Christmas were a time of elation and excitement which he felt he could hardly bear. His heart surged with happiness every time he thought of Maria. He prepared the living-room as he did every Christmas, with holly, cards, a few modest decorations and the battered-looking old Christmas tree. He spread out nuts, raisins and tangerines on the coffee-table.

He tip-toed down the stairs on Christmas morning, swaying occasionally against the banisters, his head very giddy, his heart close to bursting, and tears welling up in his eyes. He had to keep sniffing to suppress sobs of anticipation breaking from him.

When he entered the living-room, there was Maria waiting for him. She was sitting in her reclining-chair as always, with a shawl over her shoulders, her eyes brightening up at his approach. He bent over her and kissed her on the cheek, a tear falling on her forehead. He touched its wetness with a finger, as if it were holy water, swallowing harshly. He wiped his eyes, and sat down beside her. He searched for her hand as her hand searched for his.

He gripped her warm, tender flesh, and, for a few minutes, couldn't speak.

"Hello, my sweetest, sweetest darling," he said finally.

She gave a little squeeze to his hand.

They had a wonderful day, just sitting there, munching the tit-bits from the coffee-table, the television flickering away in the corner, unnoticed. Every now and then he walked away from her over to the curtains to take a peek at the snow-covered street with its street-lights, describing the scene of light and shadow to Maria. As the minutes and hours passed, he wasn't too sad, as he knew this reunion would be repeated next year, and the year after, and after that, for as long as he lived.

* * *

He puzzled over what to do for many weeks following that wonderful day. The agony of life without Maria, especially after that brief reunion, became insupportable. He had twelve months to get through before the next Christmas, and so it would go on until he died: one day of ecstasy, and then twelve months of interminable loneliness. Realizing he couldn't live so long without her, he made what he thought would be his final wish. He wished that Maria would come back again on Christmas Day, and then, after they had had another wonderful day together, he would die sitting by her side, holding hands with her. That would be heaven.

Over the next few months, wheezing and coughing, stumbling and shaking, he counted away the days to that wonderful time. He couldn't wait.

But it was never going to happen. He realized he wouldn't last until next Christmas. His dizziness was getting worse and worse. Some days he could hardly walk. Most ominously, he started to get terrible stabbing pains in his chest. He was going to die very soon. One evening he was going to go to bed and not wake up the next day. He had to change his wish for Christmas, and do so quickly before it was too late. With probably only weeks, or maybe only days of life left, this was really going to be the last wish he would ever make.

He wished that he and Maria would come alive next Christmas Day, and for every Christmas day after that. So, after a long, long blackness each year, they would draw breaths again, move their aching limbs, hold hands, and sit side by side the whole day. They would have a wonderful, wonderful time, and then, when the day was over, descend into that long, long darkness, confident that it would, eventually, end. And so it would go on until the end of time. They would sit hand in hand in their chairs in front of the television, and recall the times they had walked up and down the snow-covered street outside their house and, even earlier, the times they had run hand in hand through the glistening corn-fields of Italy and had felt that such joy could never, and would never end. Will looked forward to his imminent death with calmness and serenity. The night he would lay his head on the pillow for the last time, as all other nights, he would fall asleep with images of his beloved Maria as his one and only dream.

* * *

That Christmas Day, and every single Christmas Day afterwards, revellers, passing by that house in the snow-covered, light-and-dark street, no matter who lived in that house all the other days of the year, would report that they had espied through a chink in the curtains an old couple sitting side by side in their armchairs, neither moving nor speaking, but just holding hands and gazing at each other with enraptured eyes. Who knows? Maybe those revellers had imbibed a little too much of the Christmas spirit...Or maybe not…Maybe they were truly witnessing Will and Maria coming alive on that one day of the year when their love lived forever.

THE END
2013 Alan Hardy

A Sacred Star
By
Sheryl Seal

Prelude

I am an old woman now, but there was a time when I was youthful and owned the world. At just eighteen the world as I knew it was about to change forever. This is my story, and although I am no longer young, I have a sharp mind. I remember it all like it was yesterday and there are many days when the scenes play over in my head. That was the year that my life would forever be altered and the year we stopped celebrating the white man's Christmas.

Chapter 1

The firewood had been piled high and the cellar was stocked with foods for the winter. Papa worked hard all summer to prepare for the long cold winter months. It was already close to Christmas and the first snows had come in with blinding fury in October and never let up. We tried to live our lives like the white man and celebrating Christmas was a part of their ways. Every year since we came to live in this valley, we went into the town of Buck Meadow on Christmas to join in on their celebration. There is a giant tree which the townspeople cut down to put in the center square and everyone decorated this tree with trinkets and candles. A man who dressed up in a funny long robe and yelled Ho-Ho-Ho walked around handing out gifts to the children. I could always count on eating all kinds of sweets on this day until my belly hurt. When night came, we would stand around the tree and light the candles singing Christmas songs. I looked forward to this white man ritual every year because we could to visited with people other than ourselves.

It is always cold and snowy here in the mountains of Yosemite. That year though, seemed to be the worst winter that I could remember. My older brother was making a bow with some arrows on the dirt floor of our small cabin and I was helping mama with supper. We were having venison stew again. Mama had fairy blood running through her veins but she would not use the magic in the world of man. I wished she would so we could have something else to eat. After supper mama and papa always told stories of the old ways and how they were dying out. I had heard some fantastic tales in the eighteen years of my life. I would be eighteen soon enough, anyway. Magical things happen to the Ahwahneechee when they are in the 'Beyond' mama always said. I wanted to hear more but the time had not yet come apparently. The prophecy had foretold that I am destined for great and magical things one day. Very soon all would be revealed.

Later that night as I lay down to sleep, I heard mama and papa speak of the harsh winter. Their strained whispers came through the tiny cabin, although I tried not to listen. Mama whispered, "I hope the weather lets up soon. I worry for our families in the mountains. It is time and we need to go to the celebration this year." Papa's voice carried a little more than mama and I clearly heard him tell her not to worry so much. "All will be provided, after all, the Great Spirit has a plan.

I wondered why this celebration was so much more important than the others. We hadn't gone for years and it hadn't bothered my mama. Finally I fell asleep after tossing and turning for a while and the dreams I had were of bright colorful lights sparkling and falling all around me.

Chapter 2

The next day we had some visitors that came in with the blizzard. The storm just seemed to be getting worse. There was a pounding on our cabin door that startled us all. With the wind howling all around us, we hadn't heard anyone arriving. Papa was about to open the door when my brother chimed in, "Hey maybe it's that Santa guy!" Then he did a deep throated, Ho-Ho-Ho! Mama shushed him and moved him aside. Two fur bundled people stood at the door.

"They are freezing, let them come in and get warm," said mama. With snow falling from them, they started removing their layers and mother rushed them closer to the fire. They were shivering with the cold and I wondered how they managed to find our small cabin in the middle of nowhere in all that blinding snow.

Tall and with copper skin like us, this Indian was a very handsome man. His hair was long and the color of a dark night. There was a beautiful woman with him who was so big with child she looked as if she would burst. She was not an Indian and had skin that was of the snow and her hair was like the sun. Forgetting my manners, I stared at her because I had never seen a woman with that color of hair before. I wondered at the time where she had come from to be so far from her own people and if she missed them. She seemed to only have eyes for the Indian warrior by her side. He returned the feeling as he held her arm and helped her to sit.

They had been heading towards the mountains for the yearly celebration when the weather had slowed their travel. Although they were from the Ahwahneechee tribe papa watched them warily. The beautiful woman was called Tisayac and the warrior was named Tutokanula.

The visitors stayed for a few weeks and at night papa

played the flute and we danced and sang and Tutokanula showed us some different Indian dances. Tisayac sat with mama and sewed baby clothes chatting about the weather and telling stories about the Gods. These were amazing stories and one in particular about an Indian warrior and a Goddess who fell in love and went to live in her world. I noticed mama and papa looking at each other and he nodded and winked at her.

Later, as her stories unfolded, I learned more about the Gods and that Tisayac and Tutokanula were more than I had first thought. Theirs is a beautiful love story and now I knew why papa had given such a look and wink at mama. Their child would also be a God one day.

All of these tales felt like an old friend and although very entertaining, I found many of them strange and wondered why I hadn't heard them before now. Shape shifters were not a part of the world of man and I wasn't so sure about a Golden Queen of the Ahwahneechee either, but I knew that these stories were all part of my heritage. There is a prophecy that the Golden Queen will be one in a long line of Golden Queens to save the world from a terrible evil called the Ala. Awful as this blizzard is, nothing can compare to the havoc the Ala can cause. She will destroy any world with her evil power. It is said that the Ala looks like a big wind whirling around and consuming everything in its path. She brings with her fire and weather of every kind. She can also create many wars with man, one against the other. Only the powers of this Golden Queen will be able to save not just this world but many worlds.

Needless to say that night, I had many strange dreams. I had never had dreams like these. People were shifting into all kinds of animals and some were flying. There was a great storm threatening a whole village and for some reason, they were all looking at me like I knew what to do. Suddenly I felt warm and bright and there was blinding lights and the storm calmed. I was applauded by the villagers but for some reason, I felt a loneliness creep into my soul. With my heart pounding, I woke with a start, opened my eyes and sat up. I made out a shape standing there in the firelight and it was Tisayac. She whispered quietly in the night and I heard her words before she walked away. "You are ready now Falling Rain."

Chapter 3

The days passed by and the storm eased up and gave way to nicer weather. The snow was melting all around which was strange for this time of year. It had cleared enough and we were able to go to the big celebration. I pleaded to stay long enough for the Christmas festivities here but mama said we were in for a real celebration. "We cannot wait any longer and we need to be on our way." No amount of begging would change my mother's mind so I knew enough not to try any longer. I prepared myself for the festival ahead and hoped it would be as much fun.

We left early in the morning and traveled for two days before coming to a great water fall. "It is called Bridalveil and this is where we cross over." It had been quiet with no one talking for so long that these words spoken by Tisayac, startled me. I looked at the giant waterfall and all around. "Cross over into where? I don't see anything but water flowing down." She came to me and put her hands on my head and shifted it straight at the falls. "We go Beyond Bridalveil here." She then took my arm and guided me forward through the falls with everyone else following behind.

An Indian village set against the mountains with majestic waterfalls all around, was the sight that greeted my stunned eyes. There was no snow and it was sunny with colors so vibrant they were almost blinding. With many questions on what was happening, I looked around in wonder. A young man approached us and the first thing I noticed was how long and flowing and white his hair was. His clothes looked raggedy and his shoes looked as if they were on backwards. How he walked this way with comfort I couldn't fathom. He tweaked a piece of my very unruly auburn hair and smiled happily. "My name is Elsu and I will show you around the village." Underneath his rags he looked handsome enough. As I watched him under veiled eyes, I could see his shoes didn't bother him in the least. He did however, walk like an old man and carried a staff like one. I kept my mouth clamped tight. It was killing me not to say something about his clothing, or the fact that he pulled my hair. Smiling at him, I followed where he led.

Elsu showed us around and took us to the center where everyone was gathering for some sort of meeting.

After we were all seated, Tisayac welcomed everyone to the celebration of all life that would happen tomorrow. As she spoke it became apparent to me that it was not just mine and my brother's birthday but that it was everyone's birthday tomorrow. This could not be a coincidence. It was by design. I had been told many stories over my life and more recently in that previous week and now I am sure it was to prepare me for what would go on in this foreign place that seemed so magical.

I learned many things about my heritage and how we are all shape shifters. We would learn to shift into this spirit animal and with training we would protect the world of man from evil. It is already designed by The Great Spirit which spirit animal we will become. I could hardly wait to learn what my spirit animal is.

We slept in a lodge on fur and I woke feeling as if today was special. Of course, I was finally eighteen today. There was to be a big celebration for all of us. In my mind, I went back over everything that had happened last night and was quite surprised at how I handled everything that I had learned. Shape shifters were a part of my culture. We were brought here to learn how to help keep the world of man safe. This is a place to gain knowledge and a place of training to help us keep evil out of the world of man. On this Christmas day, I will meet my destiny.

Chapter 4

The celebration for the Christmas birthdays started off with tables upon tables of all kinds of wonderful food. There were pies of every kind, which were all my favorites and there was venison. Several birds were cooked to perfection and there was fish and many kinds of potatoes and vegetables. Where all of this food came from, I didn't have a clue, except we were told to give our thanks to Elsu. I couldn't imagine that the handsome but rather awkward guy that I had met the night before could have done all of this, but I thanked him just the same and ate a little of everything, except the venison.

In the middle of thanking him, I suddenly felt ill and my body heated up all over. "What is it Falling Rain?" Grabbing the arm of Elsu, I pinched it and said, "Don't call me that! My name is Huyana! I'm not sure, but it is something very bad. It is more than that, it is sinister and it is coming this way…" Before he could respond, the sky cracked loudly and wind ripped through the village, tearing down many lodges. Various little whirlwinds started popping up all over the village and many people started shifting into their spirit animals all around us. I had never witnessed such a thing before and it was the most amazing sight one will ever see. There were animals and birds all around me and there I stood frozen in place beside Elsu.

The sky darkened and the rain started just as a sprinkle at first and turned to a downpour very quickly. I tried to focus on everything that was happening when suddenly Elsu broke through the roar of the wind. "You will be the one to fight this evil Huyana. This is who you are, so do not fear the unknown of what will happen. You are about to defy all logic and you must listen to your instincts and ignore everything else. Ignore logic, ignore the odds, ignore the complications, and just go for it."

The villagers were scattering into the forest towards the mountain and some had not shifted yet. This was the evil that was spoken of in the prophecies and I knew it in my soul. Lightning ripped across the sky again and the village shone brightly for a moment. In that second there was an explosion and bright orbs scattered around us. I was pulled by my arm towards Elsu, who bent down and picked up one of these orbs. Before I had time to think, he thrust the bright object right into my hands and screamed over the howling wind. "This star was designed for you and will aid you in defeating the Ala and saving this world."

Chapter 5

It grew brighter and warmer as I held it in my hands and my body felt like it was on fire. I sensed the electricity run through my entire being and suddenly my body shifted into a bright blinding light and shot straight up into the sky. This certainly wasn't logical and I fearfully wondered what was happening. Then there was inner peace as this star flowed throughout my veins and released its energy. It was a powerful feeling but I didn't have much time to enjoy it because the Ala was already at the village and most of it was now on fire.

I realized that Elsu was also a glowing star beside me high in the sky and he somehow communicated with me. "This is the time of the Golden Queen Huyana; it is also the time of the Ala. There is a decision that can only come from within you. One choice will destroy the world and the other choice will break your heart." Making up my mind, I quickly chose what appeared to be the larger of the two. From all I had learned the larger one would surely destroy all worlds. The decision would cost me dearly.

As I looked down on the shifters below, I saw them take to the forest and I watched as this enormous cyclone started consuming everything in its path. It would destroy them all and everything here and then move on to other worlds. With my decision made, I let my star guide me. I surged forward and plunged at the Ala and entered into the very soul of this evil. The tortured cries from beings in other worlds were all around and waiting for release. It was these frantic pleas for help that led me on and I traveled further into the echoing mouth of the Ala.

Immediately I felt I was drowning and just when I thought I might vanish forever, I felt an electrical whirring within and an explosion of the most fantastic colors burst forth. I found myself drifting back to earth with sparkling snow slowly falling all around me. The Ala was gone and the inner peace of the star still coursed through my veins. It was mine to keep and I could call on the strength of this star whenever I needed to purge evil in the world. I was now, The Golden Queen of the Ahwahneechee.

Epilogue

There had been good and bad with the events of that Christmas day long ago. A boy child named Grey Wolf was born to Tisayac and Tutokanula. He would play a very important part of all of our lives in future generations to come.

Before that blissful event though, we had to deal with the fact that my brother was lost to us. While I was taking care of one Ala, the smaller and younger one had possessed my brother and they escaped into the world of man. Together they created fires and chaos as they traveled through Yosemite National Park. Traveling throughout the world, they spawned earthquakes and tsunamis and many other disasters.

The Dwellers of Ahwahnee were created and we changed the celebration to summer and those that have powers will come to us in this season. We still search tirelessly for my brother and the Ala and I made a vow that one day, I would bring Falling Rock home, no matter what the cost.

Little did I know that with the vow I made that day, there would be another Christmas day in the far future, where the cost might be my own granddaughter Oria...

~ ~ ~ ~

To read more about Huyana and Elsu, Grey Wolf and Oria, please read the series: Beyond Bridalveil Fall and Beyond Oria Falls (Dwellers of Ahwahnee). Their story continues...

THE END
2013 Sheryl Seal

True Heart
By
William O'Brien

And as the flakes
Crisp and white
Dance in the veil
Mist of night

Fed, now the boy
Honoured in time
Blessed and precious
No more lies

A man in the making
As depths unwind
Sincerely given
While honestly binds

The gift unexpected
Could never be imagined
Earthly goods
Now out of fashion
***

© 2013 William O'Brien

The Christmas Heart
By
Kristina Blasen

Summer (Him)

It was an unusually warm summer evening in Minnesota; anyone would tell you it was at least 80 degrees outside. Matt had just gotten off work. He was feeling tired and a little down from dealing with customers all day, but he rushed across the Twin Cities to keep a promise to a friend anyway.

When he pulled up to the house in his white jeep after work, Kristina was standing there, just staring off into space. She was wearing a rumpled t-shirt and shorts with flip flops. He only noticed her clothes since they were so far removed from the professional work clothes she wore when teaching at the college.

Her red-brown hair was clubbed back in a pony with pieces falling out every which way. He couldn't help but notice the dark smudges under her eyes made her look a little tired and sad. Sweaty dirt had left a streak across her nose and forehead where she'd rubbed her face sometime earlier in the day. He smiled to himself because he was sure she didn't know it was there.

He looked around and gave her a moment to notice him. The driveway was lined with old furniture that hopefully someone would pick up soon to save her some money on the disposal fees. The yard held the random bits and overflowing garbage cans you see whenever anyone is moving.

The aging purple minivan with its collection of dents and

rust was packed to the brim with just enough room to slide into the driver's seat. Her 10 year old son manned the front seat and his 3 year old baby sister was already locked into her carseat in the back. Kristina had graduated from the University last month. No job had turned up around here and being a single mom stuck with a house that needed two incomes to run had drained her in more ways than just financially. He knew it as her friend, but they never talked about it.

Surprisingly, she'd decided in the very last days of her lease on the house to drive across country to Florida, going back to her tiny hometown where she was never happy in the first place. But, happiness or no, she was going anyway. He didn't really understand the decision, but he would support her regardless.

She said with a brave smile that the plan was to go for the summer, to keep her options open. She was hoping for something better to turn up on the job front in a few months, something to turn around the rough patch her life had hit. They both knew she put a good face on it for the kids, but he wasn't the only one to notice how many friends didn't turn up to say goodbye.

He'd come to help move, or pack. Really, he came to say goodbye, but she was tired and worried and busy, ready to be on her way. He stood there not knowing what to say, where to look. It was awkward. He'd been her friend, shared a few casual, quick hugs over the past few years, but she was distant, didn't let people get too close. Still, there were times when they'd talk and somehow the hours would fly by for both of them.

Finally the moment had come. Reluctantly he took her into his arms, looked down into her face, then let go, stepping back quickly, firmly back into friend territory.

Goodbyes were said, half-hearted promises to keep in touch.

Thinking back on it now—there was a moment, just a glimpse of something he saw or felt, when she looked up directly into his eyes—he wondered what might have been...if. And there was something else—she had looked back. He didn't know what that meant, but it meant something, somewhere inside him. He just didn't know what to do about it.

Summer (Her)

Summer passed slowly in the forever wet, sticky heat of Southwest Florida. Kristina sat staring out the window, watching the cars pass by on the freeway just 1000 feet from her front door. She thought about those last days in Minnesota, feeling a little sad and homesick, wishing for better days from another lifetime.

The Universe laughed at her expense when the first week back in Florida a slow moving, no name tropical storm flooded the streets and took power out at the house for days. Just as they finally turned the power back on, some kid down the road ran his car into the power pole and it was right back off for another week. Should have taken the warning about what was to come the first time, she thought, remembering the end of that long drive to Florida with the minivan packed to the ceiling with stuff.

She had just crossed the state line between Georgia and Florida when a semi-truck busted a steel belted tire right in front of her. It hit and caught underneath the minivan. It was all she could do in that moment to keep the minivan under control and not flip in the center of the very first mile of Florida interstate. If that wasn't a sign leaving Minnesota was a big mistake, she didn't know what was.

She thought often of leaving Minnesota and she was terribly homesick. She hardened her resolve whenever it wavered, thinking of all her "friends" who couldn't be bothered to show up and say goodbye. To them she was already gone as soon as she said she was leaving. Sometimes it seemed like the last seven years she'd been there hadn't really mattered at all.

Kristina's family had never been close like some; her friends had been her chosen family for years now. She still had a few old friends in Florida, but she'd been gone a long time, they had their own lives and it was hard to reconnect. Since she got to Florida, she'd started a job, but it fizzled. She'd moved into a house, but it fizzled. She'd torn her heart out ending an on again, off again relationship that was never going anywhere. She wrote to friends, emailed, called, but most didn't even bother to respond. Not that she tried that hard.

I guess when things are going bad, you learn who your true friends are, she thought. Not that she really blamed all the friends who jumped ship on their friendship, no one wants to get drug down by a sinking ship and on the bad days she felt like her whole life was a sinking ship. She told herself sternly to give some credit to people, some friends had tried to help, but what was there to say? She barely made it through each day? She didn't understand how to fix it, because she didn't understand why it was broken?

Fall (Her)

Luckily, Kristina always felt better in fall. For her whole life fall brought energy, new hope, a sense of renewal. She decided to work on herself. Exercise, eating right, learning new skills, spending time writing and journaling, playing with photography, being a better mom...figuring out what was wrong with her. Some Florida friends picked her up and dusted her off. Some Minnesota friends wrote back and there was finally something good to say. Time passed.

I don't really know what changed, she thought, still remembering. One day she just started writing and talking to friends honestly—good, bad, didn't matter. Sometimes they'd write or call back, sometimes not. Some wrote back and spoke from their heart either about themselves and their life, or to encourage her. Some just never wrote back or called at all.

She smiled. Her friend Matt, he wrote back, though inconsistently. There were letters, back and forth, over time…until one day she'd told him she was coming to Minnesota to visit and asked him to lunch.

That night, she remembered, she was happy. It was a simple kind of happy that she hadn't felt in a long time, happy for time with a friend who wanted to see her. They talked that day about everything under the sun—parted happy. The next day they had lunch again, then dinner, then on to the bookstore—where they suddenly realized this felt a lot like a date—a very long marathon date.

Hugging goodbye took on a new meaning. She'd wondered at that moment if they had ever really hugged before. Sure, they must have hugged at some point in the last three years, but this felt different.

She'd looked up at him, pressed close against his shirt, her arms holding tight and realized that they had never really even seen each other before this moment. She'd almost gone up on tiptoe to kiss his cheek, his lips. She was not too shy, but she realized with a sinking heart that to follow that impulse would risk their whole friendship. It wasn't fair; she was leaving the next morning, flying back to Florida to some other life.

She let go, they parted ways. She had turned to the car, but looked back. She stood and watched him drive away until the lights of the jeep winked out of sight—only then did she wonder, what if?

If there was one thing she'd learned about Matt in three years as his friend it was that he was a good man. He truly cared about the people in his life. He was loyal and walked with honor. She'd trusted him and welcomed him into her home from the first moment they met when her best friend brought him to the door.

She couldn't remember how or why she eventually told him what she'd felt that day. She thought about it in quiet moments. Remembering flashes of other times, other moments where she'd been aware of that spark, that potential for attraction and the deep comfortableness that people get when they are good friends and already compatible.

To say sharing what she felt was out of character for her is an understatement. It was such a risk to tell him, but such joy when he said he'd felt it too. That is the real beginning of this story, it is a love story. A slow blossoming of friendship, friendship turned to caring and then to love over the course of many seasons. Like watching time lapse photography of a rose unfolding, the tiny imperceptible movements of two hearts slowly sliding together.

In the months after that first breathless and hopeful admission, the slow sweet beginnings of love took off like a match set to dry tinder. The joy and surprise, first to find love, then to finally be together. Then there was the amazement of connecting with each other on a soul deep level.

In between there was fear, hope and anxiety, mixed with caring and tenderness. Everything was somehow rushing, faster and faster leading somewhere, to something wonderful. To find joy in another, so unexpected and wonder why you never saw it before when it was right there the whole time in front of you for years. Until one day…

Winter (Us)

"I never could keep a happy secret! Your Christmas present is finally done," Matt said with a laugh in his voice.

"Show me!" Kristina laughed, shifting the phone at her ear and opening her computer to see the picture he was sending.

Soon a picture appeared on the computer screen that bridged the many miles still between them, stretching from Minnesota all the way down to Florida. Despite the distance, it was as if they sat next to each other, knees touching, hands drifting together automatically without conscious thought. It was a picture of a carved wooden heart, stained red and blue; it was beautiful, with looping scrolls and intertwined hearts. He'd spent many hours and made it with his own hands. But really, it was something different entirely, a message just between them. It was a gift, freely given. His heart. His love. A promise just for her. And she knew right away, it said everything that needed to be said between them without another word. It was just the beginning.

***

Love is a choice.
You make it every day.
When you have once loved and lost,
if you are lucky enough to find love again,
you cherish and protect it fiercely.
In order for that love to be real, to survive,
you have to give everything you are.
You take the risk.

***

"It's wonderful," she said quietly, "I love you too, Matt." He could hear her tears through the phone.

"There's more," he said softly, his voice gone gravelly with emotion. "Come home love; come back to Minnesota, to me. I'm here waiting for you. I want you and I want the kids here with me. You're the only Christmas gift I want, all of you."

THE END
2013 Kristina Blasen

This Christmas
By
Greatest Poet Alive

Perhaps I was Riley Freeman before he was even thought of by Aaron MacGruder. Yeah, I was a black kid growing up on the south side of Chicago, existing in a lower middle class environment slowly becoming gang-infested, waiting for December 25th to arrive. Christmas was a symbol of hope during a year in which I had been chased from school almost every day. Christmas was watching all of the cartoons that came on television that started right after Thanksgiving ended. Quick reflection: I always thought, until I got older, that Black Friday was an African American holiday. Don't judge me. I grew up in the city with Jesse Jackson and the famous "Keep Hope Alive" mantra. Christmas was going to plant a huge smile on my face and make life worth living for a tortured sixth grader (which is another story).

I believed in that Santa song, especially the part where it says, "He knows when you've been bad or good, so be good for goodness sake…" So, I made it my business to be good. Whatever my parents asked me to do, it got done. Take out the garbage? Done! Turn out the light at 10:00pm? I did it at 9:55pm. Make sure my homework was done, play nice with my younger brother, and come in before the street lights came on? Done!! Done!! Done!! Besides taking care of the home front, I was this close to being the "apple polisher" at school. I know Mrs. Mitchell loved me. No task was beneath me, as I cleaned the blackboards and the erasers, took Mrs. Mitchell's tray back to the lunchroom, arrived early to help staple the test papers, pass out and collect the very same test papers, and remain after school sometimes to do anything that I had not already done for Mrs. Mitchell. Whew. So if any boy, any black boy who just happened to be living on the south side of Chicago, was being good and not bad, nice and not naughty, it was me!! With that being said, all I wanted from Santa was what my cousin Derek had gotten as a whimsical gift. What was that you might be asking? The only thing on my list was a GI Joe with the Kung Fu Grip. I didn't want any vehicles. Even though there was a play set that could have come with him, I had no desire for that, either. All I needed, all I wanted, was a GI Joe with Kung Fu Grip. And darn it, I had busted my little black butt to get it. Yes, Santa, make sure you stop at 2743 East 79th Street first, and drop that off!! Oh yeah, I bought the Chips Ahoy cookies and two percent milk. You deserve only the best, Santa, and that is exactly what you're going to get. Hey, don't even mention it. Just bring the 12" inch figure with the beard to the address I put on my letter. Yep, that'll do it.

    My parents taught me never to be ungrateful, especially when it came to gifts. They said that there were always children who were worse off than my brother and I. And as much as I wanted to believe the words my parents spoke, I could not. There could not be possibly any black boy, any boy for that matter, who was worse off than me right now. Because on Christmas morning, when I raced past my brother to where the large, powdered Christmas tree stood, there were plenty of gifts. But what did I discover when I began to rip gift wrapping and tear boxes open? There was no friggin GI Joe with the Kung Fu Grip!!! My eyes were wringing out tears, which my parents mistook for joyful droplets, and I let them believe that. I didn't want to spoil it for my brother who was having a ball switching back and forth between the gifts he had sprawled out in front of him. No, I wasn't that selfish, even though I was that angry. In that moment, I knew what hatred was and who the object of it would be. I swore that I would never write another letter, acknowledge the existence of, let my sleeping pattern be dictated by, or ever put cookies and milk out for him. But more than that, I was going to get even with Santa Claus for ruining my Christmas and all the ones that would follow. Yes, I had set my mind and heart to it. Santa was going to die, and I was going to be the boy that did it.

Walking in the Evergreen Plaza Mall with my girlfriend Tabitha, I watched the long line forming where the Footlocker was down several stores past the Garrett's Gourmet Popcorn Shop ending at the center of the mall. I wondered what the reason for this long line was, and simultaneously, this very thought was answered aloud by Tabitha. Her words changed the smile that had been on my face and sent violent chills throughout my body.

"Look Baby, all those kids are waiting to see

Santa. Isn't that great?" She continued, "Hun, what do you want from Santa? You can tell me because your secret is safe."

Why did she have to point that man out to me? Why did she have to ask what I wanted, rather, still wanted decades later after the Christmas debacle? Why did he have to be at this mall at the same time Tabitha and I were here? But the most important question was not why I still hated Santa Claus. No, that wasn't it. What was I going to do about the searing sensation that inhabited my heart at the very mention of his name? As I led Tabitha away from where HE was, the answer became solid in my thoughts and would consume me going forward. Yes, that was it!!!

As soon as we arrived at Tabitha's Lake Meadows' apartment, I told her I needed space. This relationship of a little over a year was moving faster than I wanted to, is what I told her. Tabitha asked the normal questions of whether there was someone else, was I dying, etc., and so forth. And I gave her the obligatory answers. She slapped my face and sobbed uncontrollably as she exited the car without closing the door. It was all for the best because she would never understand my mission. Hell, I didn't understand it, but it had to be done!! I was going to murder Santa Claus. And with that thought taking center stage in my thoughts, I smiled and drove home.

There is no point on the map that says North Pole. To a lot of people, neither this place nor the individual I am searching for even exist. But they do, and I was going to find them. The legend goes that somewhere in Anchorage, Alaska, there was a point of an enormous mountain, and there were a series of caves that led to a lengthy tunnel where his hideout was. This information came after frequenting several seedy bars, spending thousands of dollars on drinks, and listening to ten times that many stories of good ole Saint Nick until some of the tales started to sound similar. Yes, this was a long shot. But I was a grown man who harbored intense hatred for a mythical figure. I had absolutely not a darn thing to lose, so off I went.

    The flight from Chicago to Anchorage, Alaska was close to seven and a half hours. The journey after would be longer and more treacherous. A stretch of caves, I estimated were the distance from Chicago to downtown Detroit, were my first hurdle to overcome. Then, as dehydration, exhaustion, and frostbite tried to overtake my body, I fell down a hole that seemed to have no end. My ankle was broken, fractured, or maybe severely sprained. Everything was spinning. My mouth tasted like cotton, and my stomach roared like a Tyrannosaurus Rex. Somehow though, I continued. If the journey had been any farther than it ended up being, I would have been done for. Thank goodness, the proverbial light was real and at the end of the tunnel. A mansion of Dynasty or MTV Cribs worthiness beamed with an aura of extreme wealth. Literally, I covered my eyes to shield them from being blinded. This could not possibly be the home of the evil Santa Claus!! Wait a minute!! Yeah, it could. It really could. All of that nonsense about him loving children, spreading holiday cheer, and being a great guy was all malarkey. Now, I didn't feel so bad about what I had to do. Actually, it would be a great service to all the children who sit at home writing lists and letters, being good for goodness sake, putting out chocolate chip cookies and milk, and then waking early only to find that they didn't get a GI Joe with the Kung Fu Grip. Hell Yeah!! Santa, you're about to be mine. As I walked towards the mansion, a pack of what looked like rabid reindeer attacked me. The battle was vicious and taxing on my already fatigued frame. Though I was able to fend them off, I sustained a horrible bite to my left bicep that bled profusely. I remember nothing after that, but I believe the following occurred.

*****

Dashing thru the snow (it was more like fleeing), they were right behind me. This Christmas was supposed to be different, but this is the way it turned out. I had travelled miles that encompassed half a major city's blocks, but there would be no resting or taking a breath. Those were luxuries I would have to do without. Fatigue and delirium were winning against my tenacity, so finally, and reluctantly, I give my escape a pause. I saw the elves appear in the near distance, so I renewed my sprinter's marathon. I could never let them catch me because this Christmas was to be the Christmas I murdered Santa Claus! Hours ago, the wintry wind whirled thru the air like a cracking whip. Though the Vaseline was heavily placed on my lips, it did not stop the cracking and bleeding. I wore special hiking boots on my feet to keep me from falling and incurring a fatal slip. Fearing fate would not be on my side, I felt both sides of my snowsuit begin to rip. Elves were asleep all over the workshop; it was obvious they had partied too hard. This scene reassured me that my mission's fruition was on the cards.

It figures that he was sitting there drinking brandy, feasting on a giant ham that was covered with pineapples and lard. He looked up and saw me, but gave no response as I emptied my gun, so not one bullet would I discard. I smiled with satisfaction, tucked the gun, and ran towards the hills without pause. Because a little black boy never got a G.I. Joe with Kung Fu Grip, a black man murdered Santa Claus.

I ran for twenty-five hours, but wouldn't make twenty-six. I came upon a high snow wall that wasn't there before, and I was out of escape tricks. Cornered in all directions, I made a promise to myself that I wouldn't fall. I pulled the hood of my jacket over my head, my fists both balled. The tallest of the elves with a helium-sounding voice screamed, "Do you realize what you've done?!!" He pointed to the thousand elves that surrounded me, letting me know that there was really nowhere to run. I sighed; he did the same. A revelation from his mouth was the next thing that came. He said, "Santa wasn't really Santa or St. Nick, but the Fallen Angel was his name!" My shock was palpable after the giant elf made this unholy claim. On behalf of all the elves, he thanked me vigorously, and each of the thousand told me, "You'll never know what you gave us." Before they departed, and me leaving with my life, the large elf told me that they sold their souls to the devil to be taller, "so you truly saved us!!"

THE END
© 2013 G.P.A

Secret Santa
By
Madhu Kalyan Mattaparthi

Music filtered softly through the house as a candle flickered on the mantle, casting shadows on the wall. Stockings hung flat along the wall, empty of toys and treats. A small Christmas tree sat in a corner, looking barren and sad with no toys hiding beneath the low hanging branches. There were misshapen cookies resting on a plate, alongside a glass of milk and a note addressed to Santa. A strand of lights flickered along the staircase, casting soft rays of blue, green, red, and yellow. The rest of the house was dark, save for a single light upstairs, where a shadow could be seen pacing in front of the window despite the lateness of the hour.

***

Kim came to a stop before the window. Staring out at the snow covered yard, she sighed. Pulling her robe more tightly around herself, she crossed her arms over her chest. Her lips turned into a frown and her brows pressed together. Her mind was racing with thoughts and worries, making sleep impossible. The night was slipping past Christmas Eve right into Christmas morning, a time where kids expected a bounty of toys and presents. Her children, however, would not have such a morning.

Money had been very tight lately and they were barely managing to slip by on Kim's bi-weekly pay check. This year had been especially rough, with lay-offs at the office and bills stacking up. Jessica needed a new fencing outfit, having outgrown the original starter set given by the coach upon signing up for classes. Dustin needed a new bow and quiver, having made the choice to transition from a short bow to a long bow, wanting a new challenge. Between the bills for food, electricity, heat, water, cable, phones and mortgage, Kim could occasionally afford to buy her kids some new clothing but rarely anything more. She was proud to be able to provide for her kids though, having always done her best to make sure they were well fed and clothed with a roof over their heads.

Kim stared out the window, wishing she had more money, wanting nothing more than to shower her kids with presents. They'd been so understanding and patient this year, never complaining about not being able to get the latest games or phones. It filled her with pride while breaking her heart. Kim chewed her lip as she walked towards the closet. Maybe she couldn't afford to buy a ton of presents, but she had made sure that her kids would get something. She pulled open the closet door and took out two packages; one addressed to Jessica and the other addressed to Dustin. They were both wrapped in silver-white paper.

She placed the packages on the bed, before searching for bows to place on them. She found a light blue bow, removed the sticky tape, and pushed it onto Jessica's present. She looked again and came up with an emerald green ribbon, which she placed on Dustin's present. Kim picked up the cards, that were sitting on the dresser, and placed them on top of the packages. Holding the two silver-white parcels in her arms, she walked down the hallway and crept quietly down the stairs towards the tree. She placed the packages on the couch, before taking the cards and pushing them into the top of the stockings. She then pushed the two presents beneath the tree, making sure they could be seen at first glance.

Kim sat down on the couch and watched the candle

flicker. She knew how important the fencing outfit was for Jessica and how much Dustin wanted the new bow. To make sure she could afford to get her kids these things, she'd sold her mother's watch. It was something she'd cherished, a piece of the beloved woman who had died early in Kim's young life. As special as it was, she had gone out earlier in the week and sold the jewellery to pay for the very presents she'd just placed beneath the tree; she wanted to do everything possible to make her children smile.

Kim wiped at a stray tear, while staring at the flame of the candle as it ate away the wax. The scraping of a branch against the window jarred her and she straightened, pushing the couch cushions back into place. She walked to the mantle and blew on the candle, extinguishing the flame. Kim then headed back upstairs. Walking down the hall, in the opposite direction of her room, she stopped in front of the first door and slowly turned the knob to peek into the room. A loud grunting snore greeted her, the tousled blonde hair of her thirteen year old son Dustin was just visible on the pillow. She smiled gently and eased the door shut again. Kim walked a few steps further down the hall and stopped in front of her nine and a half year old daughter's room. Kim turned the knob gently and eased the door open. The dim light from a Reindeer shaped night light welcomed her and she gazed gently at the peaceful face of Jessica. Kim walked quietly into the room. She pulled the scattered sheets up over Jessica's limp form and softly smoothed Jessica's hair, before slipping out of the room and closing the door quietly behind her.

The sight of her children sleeping so peacefully erased the sting of loss she felt over the watch and a smiled slipped over Kim's face. She would give up anything to make sure her kids were happy. She walked down the hall to her room and glanced at the clock, it was now four in the morning. She'd spent the entire night awake, worried and wondering about how to make sure this Christmas was special. Kim covered a yawn and stood in the doorway of her room. Not sure what to do now that everything was in place, she decided to finish the mystery novel she had been reading. Slipping into bed, she pulled the book out of the night-stand and opened it to the page she had last read. Settling down, she began to read.

Plink. Plink. Plink!

Kim shifted within the warmth of her blanket, wishing it would stop hailing.

Plink. Plink. Plink!

Kim groaned and peeked out from beneath the blanket. Through blurred vision, she stared hard at the window as her mind slowly realized that there was nothing but a clear, night sky beyond the glass. There was no hail or rain tapping at the window, she frowned, sitting up in bed.

PLINK!

Kim suddenly realized that someone was throwing pebbles at her window. She frowned again and threw the blanket back. Sliding her feet into her slippers and she pulling her robe back on, she walked to the window. Glancing out at the yard, she didn't see anything unusual but the pebbles hadn't been throwing themselves. She stalked down the stairs, grumbling, and yanked open the front door. Kim had been preparing to yell out at whoever was there and was so annoyed that she nearly stumbled over the bag which was sitting on her porch. She stopped, looked at the bag and then glanced around. There was a muddled array of footsteps in the snow but nobody around to claim ownership. Kim looked at the bag again and finally spied a note attached the cord that was holding the bag closed.

She detached the note. Her gaze slid over the envelope, which was a plain crepe paper. There was no writing, or markings on it. Opening the envelope quickly, the cold making her fingers shake, Kim withdrew a card. It had laughing children on the front and curving letters of script that read "Merry Christmas!" She opened the card and read the message that was printed in plain block lettering three times. Letting the meaning slowly sink in, Kim clasped a hand over her mouth; her eyes were watering. She searched the card and bag for any sign of who could have left it on her doorstep. There was nothing and she realized that the person didn't want to be known.

She gripped the bag and pulled it inside. Sitting down heavily on the couch, she stared at the card. It read simply: I know how hard you've been working this year, how hard you try to make your children happy. Things have been hard for you, and I want to help. So I've left this gift for you, and hope that it helps you. Merry Christmas. Keep being an amazing mother. Kim set the card on the coffee table and pulled the bag towards her. Glancing within, she had to bite her lip to stop from crying out. The bag was full of toys and gifts, divided equally for each child. There was an array of gifts: book, skates, board games and more. There was also a little golden bag with a tag on it that read in red script: Kim. Kim gripped the bag and withdrew it. Staring at it, she slowly pulled apart the string and withdrew a plain black box. With shaking fingers, Kim opened the box slowly and felt such shock that she nearly dropped it. Inside was a slip of paper that read: I know how much this meant to you and that you sacrificed it for your family. I hope it makes you smile. Inside the box, shining brightly against the velvet lining, was her mother's watch. She couldn't speak, tears spilled from her eyes and gratitude flooded through her.

The stairs creaked and Kim turned to see Jessica and Dustin standing at the bottom of the staircase. Jessica ran to her.

"Mommy, are you okay? Don't cry, everything is alright," Jessica said, hugging her tightly. She rubbed the tears off of her mother's face, which made Kim laugh.

"I know baby, it's alright, mommy is crying because she is happy." Dustin came over and fell onto the couch next to them.

"Crying because you're happy? That doesn't even make sense," he said. Kim smiled and ruffled his hair.

"Maybe not, but don't think about it too much. Are you ready to open presents?" Kim's voice with bright with excitement, knowing it would encourage the kids to be more excited.

"Yes," Jessica yelled out, clapping her hands.

"Sure," Dustin grinned. Kim got up and sat Jessica down. Gazing at her kids with love, she pulled the bag into view.

"Santa sure brought a load of presents this year for you guys! Take a look."

Kim backed away as Jessica and Dustin began digging in the bag, yelling with excitement at the gifts. Kim felt a surge of joy at seeing the happiness on their faces and sent a quick prayer of thanks to whoever might be up above listening. She had a feeling this might be their best Christmas yet.

THE END
2013 Madhu Kalyan Mattaparthi

Time To Go
By
William O'Brien

In the room of
Mystical trades
Spells press through
Creating doorways

Pixies, star-elves
Take to the floor
Frosty ice crystals
Stick to the door

Witch and a wizard
A small smelly man
Glowing in the room
As only fairies can

The world of crazy
Little makes sense
Bizarre, disturbed
Look over the fence

Revealing a love
Along the way
Touches the heart
Tale for another day!
***

© 2013 William O'Brien

About The Authors
Madhu Kalyan Mattaparthi
Sheryl Seal
Alan Hardy
William O'Brien
Sonya C. Dodd
Chris Raven
D.C Rogers
Peter John
Jim Murdoch
James Gordon
Kristina Blasen
Shemeka Mitchell
Carolyn Bennett

*
***
*

Find Us On Facebook

William O'Brien

Living in a small village in Lancashire, England, William O'Brien has written his second book, Peter, Enchantment and Stardust. In the 1990s, the author had twenty-one articles published, both nationally and internationally. After gaining an honours degree in Geosciences, doing post-graduate study in Occupational Health and Fitness, and earning a masters degree in Science Communication, he developed an interest for simple communication. A passion for writing again emerged, and combining various interests in fine art, museum exhibition display, biology, geology, poetry, and the mystical led to the story of Peter: A Darkened Fairytale. The author still retains a childlike vision of the world, which is conveyed throughout his books.

Also By William O'Brien

Madhu Kalyan Mattaparthi

Madhu Kalyan Mattaparthi is an IT professional from Hyderabad, India, born on 16th January 1989. He is a philanthropist, traveller and pursues writing as a hobby. Sensitive and observant, everything that happens around him is an inspiration to do something new. His knowledge in the world of technology has earned him appreciation and success and he now considers writing his new passion. He has worked in Google, India as a CEA and also the owner of a start-up company, Green Turtle Software Solutions.

Also By Madhu Kalyan Mattaparthi

Sheryl Seal

Sheryl Seal, with her husband of 30 years lives in Greeley Hill, California, a gateway to Yosemite National Park. I write Paranormal/Fantasy and I am currently working on a series of ghost stories. With six children and six grandchildren life has been full of fairies, dragons, shape shifters, and a whole world full of magic where there's still hope for a new generation of young readers.

Also By Sheryl Seal

Alan Hardy

Alan Hardy: I'm a Brit. Director of an English language school for foreign students. Married, with one daughter. Poet and novelist. Poetry pamphlets: Wasted Leaves, 1996; I Went With Her, 2007. Comic, bawdy novel GABRIELLA available on Amazon as Kindle e-book. Other novels, similarly disrespectful, surreal and shocking, on their way. Get ready for them.

Also By Alan Hardy

Gabriella
Alan Hardy

A World of Romance by ASMSG Authors
A Short Story Collection

A World of Possibility
by The Authors Of ASMSG
Short Story Collection

A World of Verse
by ASMSG Authors
A Poetry Collection

Sonya C. Dodd

Sonya C. Dodd lives in Norfolk, England with her husband and two sons. Although Sonya began writing in 1996, it wasn't until 2013 that she started to publish her work. A teacher, as well as a mother and writer, Sonya has a selection of novels and short story collections available.

Also By Sonya C. Dodd

Chris Raven

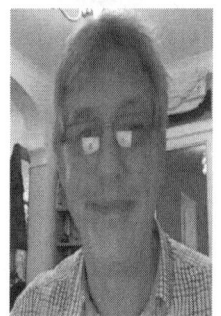

Chris Raven is a forty-odd year old south Londoner, with the emphasis on the 'odd'. He is a relative new comer to writing fiction and he is currently experimenting with a number of different formats and genres, including short storytelling and play writing. Chris has also contributed illustrations to other writer's works and he has been coordinating a shared writing project with other new writers (nominally called "Tall Stories") but more about that later no doubt.

Also By Chris Raven

Dead Shambles

D C Rogers

Author D C Rogers is a 31 year old man with ideas people say are great so he's decided to write them down. Hailing from the deep dark valleys of Wales, where his first zombie based novel stems, he lives happily with his fiancé. Pretty new to the game of writing his style is fast and fresh, focusing on thrillers horrors and fantasy works. I just want to show you lot the chaos in my mind!

Also By D C Rogers

Peter John

Peter John was born in Bromley Kent, England in 1973. He gained an interest in creative writing at the age of 14 and was published during the 1990s in several poetry anthologies. Happily Married to Jo since 1996 and currently living in Sidcup Kent, not so far from the tree.

Also By Peter John

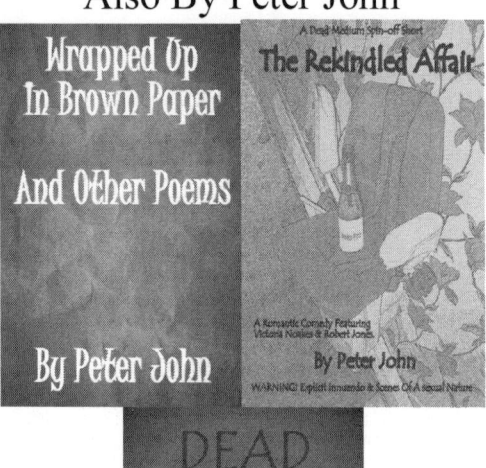

Jim Murdoch

From Belfast, Northern Ireland, Jim Murdoch faced a paradigm shift which gave him a new world view. He views everything and everyone as being connected. A path of self development studies followed where he delved into many subjects including metaphysics and, yes, dragons. With his wife, Katharina, he co-authored their self-help story Wings of Change. This got him thinking about writing fiction instead of boring self-help books. Taking inspiration from The Alchemist and The Celestine Prophecies he waited for the inspiration. The book you are holding is the result. Jim lives with his wife in Switzerland.

Also By Jim Murdoch

Greatest Poet Alive

G.P.A. is a multi-award winning Poet and author. He has written four books of Poetry(The Confessional Heart of a Man, The Book of 24 Orgasms, The Mind of a Poetic Unsub, and the Poetry Book of the Year, Revenge of the Orgasm). G.P.A. has won the Poetry Pentathlon, Moth Storytelling Slam, and the Urban Image Magazine Talent Search.

Also By The Greatest Poet Alive

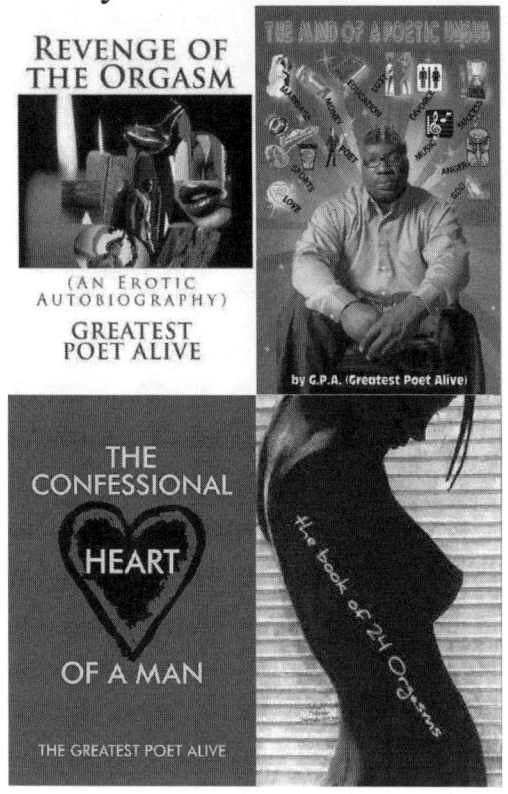

Kristina Blasen

Kristina Blasen is a dabbler. She writes a dab of this and a bit of that. She enjoys writing children's fantasy, short stories and poetry. Her dark fantasy short story collection, Tales of the Wyrd, is her favorite collection. She's also the author of three poetry chapbooks: The Wildwood Guardian, Grey Weir and Slipshod Mornings & Meandering Midnights and is currently finishing her first full length novel, a science fiction fantasy called Gateways through the Penumbra.

Also By Kristina Blasen

Shemeka Mitchell

Shemeka has always had stories playing themselves out in her head. As a child, she wouldn't go anywhere without a pen and a notebook to write it all down. As much as she loved writing; she loved reading more. Books were her best friend in growing up and continued being that in adulthood. She is the mother of two and an advocate for Lupus Awareness. One day, after listening to her good friend, David, go on and on about all of the different adventures that he had experience, she made up her mind to finally live her dreams and publish a book. Her dear friend encouraged her every step of the way. His best advice to her was "Do what you love and remember that you do it because you love it!" Then began her journey of becoming an Author!

Also By Shemeka Mitchell

Carolyn Bennett

Carolyn Bennett lives in Ontario, Canada. A widowed mother of one son, Carolyn has always had an interest in the paranormal. In 2010 joined Canadian Haunting and Paranormal Society (CHAPS) as an investigator. Her first big investigation was at Waverly Hills Sanatorium in Louisville Kentucky. In 2011, Carolyn resigned from investigating but never lost her love for the hunt. In 2012 she began writing paranormal stories in order to fill the void left behind after leaving CHAPS. In 2013 the first novel in her series of paranormal mysteries was published, she returned to her home town of Pembroke, Ontario and rejoined the paranormal team.

Also By Carolyn Bennett

Other Publications by The Indie Collaboration
Tales From Dark Places: The Halloween Collection

A selection of chilling stories from some of the best Indie authors on the market. We dare you to venture into these pages of spine chilling tales and stories of ghosts and goblins. Freely donated by the authors themselves, these dark passages are a great example of their various, unique styles and imaginations. This is the first of a series of free topical collections brought to you by The Indie Collaboration.

***

Made in the USA
San Bernardino, CA
14 December 2013